$10.95

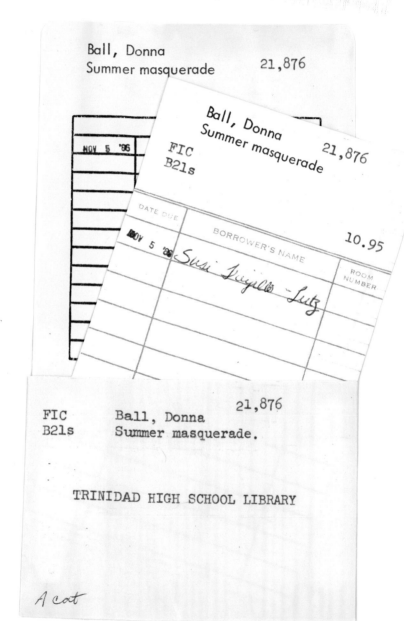

Ball, Donna
Summer masquerade   21,876

NOV 5 '95

Ball, Donna   21,876
Summer masquerade

FIC
B21s

10.95

DATE DUE	BORROWER'S NAME	ROOM NUMBER
NOV 5 '95	Susi Virgils - Lutz	

FIC   Ball, Donna   21,876
B21s   Summer masquerade.

TRINIDAD HIGH SCHOOL LIBRARY

A cat

Summer Masquerade

Summer Masquerade

DONNA BALL

DOUBLEDAY & COMPANY, INC.

GARDEN CITY, NEW YORK

1982

All of the characters in this book
are fictitious, and any resemblance
to actual persons, living or dead,
is purely coincidental.

Library of Congress Cataloging in Publication Data

Ball, Donna.
Summer masquerade.

I. Title.
PS3552.A4545S9   813'.54
AACR2
ISBN 0-385-17828-X
Library of Congress Catalog Card Number 81–43285

First Edition

Summer Masquerade

CHAPTER 1

Annabelle Morgan was not a vain girl, and certainly could not have held her peaceful position in the charitable household of her aunt had she been given to envy, but now, viewing herself in the full-length glass, she had to recognize a slight twinge of secret jealousy that the rose satin gown she was modeling belonged to her cousin Lucretia and not to herself. She was standing on a hassock while Lucretia knelt below her, her mouth full of pins, busily turning and folding the thick ruching to reveal a daring four inches of Annabelle's serviceable house slippers, flirting dangerously with the ankle. Lucretia insisted her new gown should be in the absolute latest fashion for the Wordsbury ball at the end of the month, and the latest fashions, despite her scandalized mother's protests, were quite short.

"What do you think, Bella?" demanded Lucretia, for her vantage point from the floor was poor.

Annabelle turned this way and that, noticing how the vibrant color set off her ivory skin and made her dark curls shine. It would do the same for Lucretia. In figure and coloring they were very much alike. "It will knock Freddy's eyes right out of his head," she pronounced.

Lucretia almost swallowed a pin in laughter. "Bella, don't be so vulgar! What if Mama should hear?"

"She would say it's all those trashy novels I read and despair of me once again." She stepped down from the stool, with a final, longing, backward glance at the mirror, and then said briskly, "Unhook me, then, and I'll get to work on it this afternoon."

Swiftly, Lucretia threw her arms around her. "You are the dearest, sweetest cousin who ever lived and I don't know what Mama and I ever did before you came to live with us! You know I can't sew a stitch and I would simply *mangle* it." With one of those swift, unprovoked changes of mood and subject which were characteristic of her conversation, Lucretia's face fell. "Oh, I *do* wish you were going too, you do know that, don't you? It will be such fun and I think it's simply too, too bad—"

"Pooh!" Annabelle waved it away with genuine distaste. "It will be a crashing bore and you couldn't drag me there." Then, because she caught a hint of injury in her young cousin's expressive dark eyes, she added quickly, "But it's what you enjoy, so I wish you the very best of times. And don't worry about me; I've been on the shelf for years. No self-respecting matron in the county would invite an old maid to her spring ball!" Even if the old maid were not outspoken, opinionated and living off the charity of relatives.

But now Lucretia did look worried. "But you're only twenty-six!" she exclaimed, as though the thought had just occurred to her. "I'll be that in another six years! Oh, Bella—you don't suppose—you don't think—"

"Of course not!" returned Annabelle in gentle exasperation. "You and Freddy will be married with half a dozen children long before then!" Then, as the bell rang downstairs, "There's the post—your invitation will be in it, I'll wager."

Cheered as only one with her childlike temperament could be, Lucretia flew down the stairs and Annabelle stepping carefully down from the hassock, was left to try to undo the stubborn hooks herself.

Annabelle had no reason to feel sorry for herself, though many in her position would have looked for one. She blessed the day Aunt Mildred and Uncle Jonas had rescued her from the prospect of a dreary governess' post for which her orphaned state had destined her. From the time she was admitted into their household as companion to her personable young cousin Lucretia, living on the fringe of the fashionable world of lords and ladies in which they moved, there had never been a dull moment, never the slightest lack of material with which to fill her voluminous journals, and no rein drawn on Annabelle's fertile imagination. If she could have felt sorry for anyone, it would have been Lucretia, for whom the untimely death of her father just as she was about to be presented to society had ended forever any aspirations toward taking her rightful place in the London *ton*. But it had all worked out very well. They had lived in retirement at Arnsworth Hall for the past two years, where Lucretia had promptly fallen in love with the noble Freddy and couldn't have been happier. And Annabelle, through the gossip gleaned from Aunt Mildred and her London friends, never lacked for material for her little scribblings—an enterprise which she had only recently discovered could be turned to profit.

It had been a streak of pure devilment that prompted

Annabelle to turn a collection of her wry observations and gossipy tales into a novel and to send it to a London publisher. She never truly believed that anyone would pay good British sterling for what she wrote. But the publisher had done exactly that, and further, her little volume had been the talk of the town since it was first released three months ago, and she had another novel of the same type half finished already. The only drawback to her newfound success was that she must keep her authorship strictly secret, even from the members of her own family. Aunt Mildred would never have approved of her charge pursuing so unladylike an occupation as that of a novelist and not by any stretch of the imagination was she likely to approve the sort of thing Annabelle wrote.

Lucretia flew back through the door at that moment, waving a handful of envelopes, and exclaimed, "It came!" She sank to the bed and read breathlessly, "You are cordially invited to partake of supper and ballroom dancing at Wordsbury Park, seventeen July, in the year of our Lord eighteen hundred sixteen, at nine o'clock P.M." She sighed and pressed the card romantically to her breast.

"Good," said Annabelle. "Now you can unhook me before I spoil your dress. Remember not to sit down in it or you'll never get the wrinkles out."

Lucretia giggled, flipping through the envelopes. "I've no intention of sitting at the ball, but how I'll get there I don't know, unless you expect me to fly."

"Lucy, please, it's hot." Annabelle backed up before her and Lucretia absently began to unfasten hooks as she opened another envelope. "You shouldn't read your mother's mail," Annabelle cautioned over her shoulder.

"I don't see why not," returned Lucretia. "You know she's only going to ask one of us to read it to her anyway."

"Poor thing," agreed Annabelle. "Her sight is going rapidly, I'm afraid, and she refuses to admit it." Carefully, she bent her knees so that Lucretia could reach the top buttons. "Anything important?"

"No," murmured Lucretia, "just one of her stuffy old friends . . . Lady Marbrough . . ." She started to fold the paper and then suddenly caught her breath, her eyes widening as they rapidly scanned the lines. "Oh, *no!*" she whispered.

"What is it?" Annabelle turned, but Lucretia only held out the letter to her and managed again, "Oh, no!"

Annabelle read it out loud, curious, but with little intonation, rapidly, "Dearest Mildred, hoping this missive finds you well, et cetera, et cetera . . ." She skimmed over the amenities. Nothing there to cause the alarm which registered still in Lucretia's face. "To the point of this letter"—there Annabelle stopped and glanced up briefly—"To the point . . . It is my growing concern for your lovely young daughter Lucretia, still in the first blush of her youth yet so poorly wasted on that dreary country society you love! My dear, surely you know no one sympathizes with your loss more acutely than I, but you have been in mourning two full years—an eternity for a young girl I am certain—and you must consider your responsibilities. Poor dear Jonas would not have wanted you to neglect his only daughter's future through your own sorrow, great though it may be.

"I do certainly appreciate your reluctance to bring her out in London and wish you to be assured I think you quite right on that score, indeed, most proper, which is why I think the little holiday I have planned in Brighton is just the thing. I wish to invite Lucretia to join me there in a fortnight's time."

Annabelle looked up. "Why—that's wonderful! What a marvelous opportunity—"

Lucretia shook her head, covering her eyes with her hand. "Oh, no, no," she moaned. "You don't understand . . . Besides, read on."

Annabelle scanned the page, found her place, and continued, "Before you decline too hastily, let me remind you that Brighton is not at all like London, so it would not be as though she were entering society in its proper sense, you understand. It would merely be a quiet summer's pleasure for a young girl too long confined. I am convinced both she and I would find it most enjoyable.

"Further, my dear, because I think we are close enough to be frank I must point out that the poor girl is not getting any younger. Some decision must be made regarding her future soon. To this end, I plan, with your permission of course, to make her known to my nephew, Devon Lanson. You will remember he is my cousin Elvira's boy, who married Lord Simmington. He is a very fine young man, I assure you (though perhaps I should not say 'young,' as he will see his thirtieth birthday next March) and of the best of families as you know, but unfortunately, he is a second son with no expectations to speak of. That is what put me immediately in mind of Lucretia. I feel certain a match could be arranged if you are agreeable.

"I will write more on this subject later, but first only say she may come and my mind will be much relieved.

"With all my fondest regards I remain your most loving friend . . ."

Annabelle looked up. "Well," was all she could say.

Lucretia lay back on the bed, her hand pressed dramatically to her forehead, and cried, "Oh, my life is ruined! Don't you see? Don't you know what this means? Oh, how could she?"

"I don't see that she has done anything but to make you a most generous offer for a summer at Brighton," replied Annabelle sensibly, folding the letter. "And what's more, I'm sure your mama will say yes, so I really don't see anything to go into vapors about."

Lucretia sat up straight on the bed, her eyes tearful. "I know she will say yes," she cried. "That is what's so awful! Annabelle," she demanded, "how *can* I go to Brighton just now when Freddy—when it is that awful lady's intention to see me married to that nephew of hers and when Freddy—"

"Oh," replied Annabelle, beginning to understand. "As for that—you needn't marry him, you know. You only need *meet* him. And enjoy the remainder of your holiday."

"I know Mama will insist I go," Lucretia moaned, "once she reads that letter. Or make me feel like an ungrateful child the rest of my life." She looked up pitifully. "She isn't overfond of Freddy, you know, but she has only just come to accept him thinking he may be the only offer I'm likely to get. When she hears of this nephew of her dearest friend . . . she'll never be satisfied with less, never! And the worst part, Annabelle, is that I think Freddy is coming to the point—no, I'm sure of it! He intends to ask for me at the Wordsbury ball. And if I am not there . . ."

"If you are not there," Annabelle assured her, "he will wait." But she sat down, still wearing Lucretia's gown but now heedless of wrinkles, and her brow furrowed thoughtfully. "I think you're right, you know," she said. "Aunt Mildred will surely press this match when she hears of it. Family connections mean so much to her—the fact that he hasn't a fortune won't matter a whit."

"And she will never, ever give her blessing to Freddy if she knows this Lanson person is still available! Oh, how *could* this happen? How *could* it?"

"That is true," agreed Annabelle.

"We could destroy the letter," suggested Lucretia hopefully, "and never tell her . . ."

Annabelle gave her a look of shocked reproval which spoke for itself. "Besides," she added, "Lady Marbrough would only continue writing, and you would be found out, sooner or later."

Lucretia sank back, despair filling her eyes once more.

"I'll tell you what I would do," said Annabelle with sudden decision, and Lucretia turned to her as though to an oracle. "I would go and do everything in my power to make certain Mr. Lanson never offered for me. I would be obnoxious and spoiled and simple-headed and rude . . . he would be well glad to be rid of me! And so would Lady Marbrough. And," she added, "it is the only way you will ever be rid of the two of them and their notions."

"Oh," sighed Lucretia, "you are so clever, Annabelle! But I could never do all those things! I would be mortified! I simply couldn't."

Annabelle had to agree she did not have it in her.

"Besides," Lucretia continued earnestly, "I simply must be here for the Wordsbury ball, don't you see? I can't simply fly the county when Freddy is to the point . . . It would look as though I didn't care!"

"Shh," cautioned Annabelle as Aunt Mildred's pattering steps were heard upon the stairway. "Say nothing for the moment—I will think of something!"

Self-consciously, Annabelle hid the letter behind her as her mother fluttered through the doorway.

"I do declare," she exclaimed, her violet eyes round in a soft face, her black-swathed bosom rising and falling rapidly as she pressed a small bound volume to it. "I have never been so scandalized in my life! When Maybelle Anderson read to me from this, I simply could not believe my ears! I do swear it has practically sent my head reeling and I have misplaced my hartshorn—Lucretia, my dear, have you yours about you?"

"Gracious," declared Lucretia in a somewhat falsetto voice, "what has set you about so?"

Her mother held the volume out dramatically. "This —novel—this abomination—this trash! Oh, dear, I think I will swoon!"

Annabelle, though in severe doubt that the stout lady

would ever come near to doing anything of the sort,
made a great show of hurrying to help her to the nearest
chair, fanning her with the hastily snatched invitation.
Weakly, Lady Arnsworth smiled and then, recovering
quickly, said, "Why, Lucy, how fetching you look in
your new gown! The color does become you, as I was
sure it would, though I can't help wishing it were not
quite so bold . . ." She turned to Lucretia, still sitting
upon the bed. "What do you think, Annabelle?"

Annabelle smiled patiently. It was a mistake the befuddled lady had made more than once. "No, Aunt
Mildred, it is I. Lucy was simply pinning up the gown
while I modeled it."

In confusion, Lady Arnsworth looked from one to the
other and then laughed deprecatingly, "Silly me! But
you two do grow more alike every day!"

Annabelle said, "So do tell what can be in that little
book to put you in such a state?" She made a move to
take it from her, but Lady Arnsworth clasped it more
firmly to her bosom.

"Indeed no! I will not have my innocent girls corrupted by such trash!"

"Surely, ma'am," insisted Annabelle, "our delicate
sensibilities can be no more easily corrupted than your
own. Is it banned?"

"It should be!" declared Lady Arnsworth haughtily.
"And Lord Appleby intends to sue, I heard that just the
other day! Imagine—referring to him as a plucked pea-
cock as he struts about town in his new pantaloons!
Lord Appleby!"

Annabelle stifled a giggle. "Why, ma'am, that strikes

me as strangely similar to a comment your friend Caroline Wimple made when she wrote from London not long back."

Lady Arnsworth gave an uncomfortable grunt. "It is one thing, my dear, to make such confidences in a letter and quite another to have them published abroad for all the world to read."

"Surely the author doesn't use real names?"

"No, but closely enough disguised so that there is no mistaking, I can assure you!"

"I doubt Lord Appleby will sue, then," decided Annabelle wisely. "He would hardly do so without admitting that he was the reference in the book and that would be rather embarrassing for him, I think."

"Perhaps," Lady Arnsworth agreed reluctantly, "but there ought to be a law . . ." She broke off suddenly, her eyes lighting as she spied the invitation in Annabelle's hand. "Oh, has the post come already? Was there anything for me?"

"Only the invitation to the Wordsbury ball," began Annabelle uncomfortably, and unexpectedly Lucretia broke in.

"And the most exciting thing, Mama, from Lady Marbrough," she declared and whipped out the letter as Annabelle turned on her in astonishment. "I'm sure Annabelle is reluctant to mention it to you for fear you would say no, but really, Mama, it is the most marvelous opportunity for her and she has been so good to us!"

"Dear heavens," exclaimed Lady Arnsworth, sitting up with interest, "what can it be?" Annabelle was speechless.

"Lady Marbrough," continued Lucretia avidly, "is taking her holiday in Brighton this summer and wishes to know if you could spare Annabelle for the duration as her companion. Just think how exciting it would be for Annabelle, and you have raved so much about how pleasant she is that Lady Marbrough immediately thought of her. And don't think she cannot go because she has no clothes because I will make my wardrobe open to her, and oh, Mama, it would be too cruel and ungrateful of you to say she must not go!"

Lady Arnsworth, somewhat overwhelmed, murmured, "I shouldn't dream of it! Of course she must go! How—very delightful for you, Annabelle." She beamed. "Didn't I always tell you virtue had its reward? And you will like my friend Lady Marbrough—such a charming person. She will not be the least burden upon you, I am sure, and—oh, how very kind of her. We must write a suitable reply immediately!" She rose. "I'll have tea brought to the morning room while we compose one. Come along, girls. My, isn't this exciting?"

But the two girls lingered behind, Annabelle accusing, Lucretia guiltily. "It came to me all at once," she blurted as soon as her mother was out of hearing, "when she made that mistake about us—that no one I am likely to meet in Brighton has seen me for ages and you could very easily pass for me . . . Oh, Bella, you *will* do it, won't you? Go to Brighton in my stead and discourage that horrible Lady Marbrough and her nephew?"

"Go," replied Annabelle, stunned, "as you?"

"Yes, yes," replied Lucretia enthusiastically. "You can do it, Bella, I know you can! And you always did love playacting—think what fun it will be! And"—with great courage, she tossed in the final inducement—"I will even let you take my new gown."

Slowly, Annabelle turned away. To enter firsthand the society she had only viewed from a distance all these years, to play the greatest of jokes upon them all, to be in the midst of it, rather than on the fringe . . . what a smashing new book that would make. And what an adventure!

The daring in her would not let her refuse.

She turned with a smile, and extended both her hands. "Yes," she said, "I will go."

CHAPTER 2

"Miss Arnsworth." And again, more loudly, "Miss Arnsworth."

Annabelle turned with a guilty start, fighting back a blush. That was the second time today she had made that mistake. The first had been when Lady Marbrough's doorman had welcomed her as "Miss Lucretia Arnsworth, of course" and she had almost corrected him. She had bitten her tongue just in time, and already she was beginning to see the impossible folly of the adventure she and Lucretia had concocted between them.

It was the seventeenth of June and Annabelle had only just arrived in Brighton. The three months of summer stretched formidably ahead when she considered all the obstacles in the face of the charade.

The housekeeper, Braddock, waited somewhat impatiently at the door and Annabelle inclined her head pleasantly. "I'm sorry, I must have been dreaming. What is it?"

She imagined faint suspicion in the plump woman's eyes. "Lady Marbrough, miss, sends her apologies for the delay and suggests perhaps you would like to freshen up before tea while she attends to—some rather unexpected business."

"Yes, of course."

Rather flustered, she gathered up her gloves and reticule and followed the woman out of the parlor and toward the polished staircase in the hall, her mind flitting in a thousand directions. How very simple and exciting it had seemed when she and Lucy had put their heads together over it only last evening, smoothing out the last details, assuring each other with giddy camaraderie of the ease of success. What an adventure it had seemed then, what a harmless little farce! Lady Marbrough had not seen Lucretia since infancy and could not possibly be expected to mark the difference between her and her more mature cousin. Lucretia had been in virtual seclusion since her father's death and it seemed quite unlikely that any of her old friends would recognize her now. There seemed no conceivable reason why Annabelle should not be able to happily pass herself off as her cousin for the summer and have a great deal of fun in the doing.

But the scheming was quite different from the action, and already Annabelle was beginning to suspect the little masquerade had not started out very well. First there had been the rain, miraculously disappearing as soon as the Arnsworth Hall coach reached Brighton, but accounting for just enough lost time to delay their arrival and put the housekeeper in an uncomfortable temper. It perhaps accounted as well for the disruption in Lady Marbrough's schedule, for Annabelle did not think it customary for a hostess to keep a houseguest waiting in the parlor for almost half an hour before being shown to her room. And that brought on a flood of unwelcome but inevitable anxieties and fears: What if, through

some divination unforeseen, she had already been discovered as an imposter? What if *that* were the cause of
her hostess' delay—the "unexpected business" to which
the housekeeper referred? Her heart sank as she
climbed the stairs so that she took no note of the elaborate surroundings or the direction in which they were
proceeding. Suppose the coachman, refreshing himself
and his horses at this very moment, chanced to make
some offhand reference to "Miss Annabelle" to one of
the other servants, and the remark at this moment was
traveling like a spark on a fuse toward the house? What
if, through some unimagined circumstance, her own
aunt had learned of the deception and had posted a letter which was even now traveling the same road she had
taken . . . what if a thousand, thousand horrors had
made themselves manifest, and how could she ever have
allowed herself to be persuaded to undertake anything
so foolish?

The charade was precisely the sort of thing one could
expect from the flighty Lucretia, but she, Annabelle
Morgan, a mature and independent woman, should
have known better.

"I hope this will be satisfactory, miss." The housekeeper opened the door on a spacious, delightfully
furnished room in sprigged green and pink, and Annabelle drew an appreciative breath.

"Quite satisfactory," she answered and stepped inside.

Though the Arnsworth chambers were similarly furnished, Annabelle had stubbornly refused to allow any
extravagance to be made for her benefit. Her own
room at home was simple and utilitarian, and she had

often secretly looked down her nose at the lavish frills and furls which decorated Lucretia's bedchamber and at the rich satins and velvets which furnished her aunt's. Simplicity, she maintained, was necessary for a clear mind, and when she was writing she had no patience with distractions in her surroundings. But now she thought the pleasantly feminine chamber, with its pink brocaded sitting area and ruffled canopy bed, would be quite refreshing, and perhaps not distracting at all.

"Tea is served in half an hour," added Braddock. "Punctual." Annabelle did not know whether the emphasis on this last word was for her benefit or her hostess'. "Your things are already unpacked, miss. Will you be needing a girl to help you change?"

"No," said Annabelle quickly, anxious to be accommodating. She gave a high little laugh she had carefully acquired from Lucretia. "It *is* so awkward of me to have left my girl at home, but the silly thing came down with a nasty head cold just as we were to leave. I knew she would be no use to me at all, for she does make such a *bother* of such things." Lucretia's maid was even more scatterbrained than Lucretia was herself, and she would have been certain to make some slip.

Braddock nodded, unimpressed, and turned toward the door. "The bell's by the bed, miss, if you change your mind."

Annabelle smiled and nodded and was relieved to be left alone.

With a sigh, she carefully removed her bonnet with its alluring little clump of violets on the brim and sat down on the bed. She had a half an hour to gather her thoughts and prepare for the most incredible scene of her life—that in which she would try to convince her aunt's oldest and most respected friend that she was the very wealthy and very eligible Lucretia Arnsworth and not, in fact, her older and poorer cousin. And the time would best be spent with action, and not anxiety.

Lucretia, simple and generous soul that she was, had insisted upon supplying her cousin with an entirely new wardrobe for the occasion. After all, she had pleaded with her mother, Annabelle would be seen in the smartest places with the most fashionable people and must certainly dress the part. Her mother, though not a pinchpenny by any means, had labored in some puzzlement over this, feeling certain it was not Lady Marbrough's intention to introduce Annabelle to society; rather, Annabelle's role would be merely as companion to the older woman for the summer. Lady Arnsworth even went so far as to suggest writing at once to clear the matter up, at which point Lucretia hastily conceded that perhaps it was not like traveling to London after all and that the wardrobe need not be quite so extensive. The result included two morning dresses, one of sunflower-yellow gauze dotted with pale pink roses at the bodice, another of lavender muslin trimmed with dove-gray ribbons; three of the most charming walking ensembles Annabelle had ever seen; and, in addition to the rose evening gown which was Lucretia's gift to her, an apple-green confection trimmed with yards of white netting and fashioned in the very latest Parisian style.

Annabelle, whose diligent eye had been ever watchful over the household budget, fought a hard battle with her conscience over incurring such expenses without protest, but she did not regret her silence. It was all very well to keep to dove-gray and navy-blue silk when one's primary duties included entertaining silly old colonels and dowager wives, but a great deal depended upon her now being able to look the part of the frivolous Lucretia Arnsworth. At least she had been able to talk her cousin out of the lacy whites and baby pinks which were Lucretia's choices in favor of colors and styles more suitable to Annabelle's bearing, and she did not regret her selections.

She chose for her first meeting with her hostess an aqua blue afternoon dress with a single fall of white lace about the shoulders. Her dark ringlets, a little crushed from the journey, required some repair, and at the dressing-table glass she pulled a back knot of hair high up on her head, allowing a few curls to escape and trail randomly about her cheekbones with an alluring but sophisticated dash. Around her throat she clasped an unornamented dark velvet ribbon, and it was the perfect touch. At last she stood and turned to the large gilt-framed pier glass to scrutinize her work.

The Empire style was designed for women with slender, small-waisted figures like hers. Her aunt, along with most of her generation, considered the fashion outrageous, leading, she declared, to loose conduct and an ultimate degeneration of the country's morals. But Annabelle had already seen several young ladies similarly adorned since her arrival in Brighton, strolling or chatting in the backs of open carriages, and she knew she had been quite right in insisting the fashion was respectable. In any case, she doubted very much if she could have given up the charming gown for anyone's wishes.

The soft fabric fell from a cluster of white ribbons at the bodice and swept about her ankles, just revealing the tips of new satin pumps. The bodice itself was somewhat daring, revealing a little more bosom than was perhaps strictly customary as it dipped to meet the ribbons, but the affect was easily offset by the cape of demure lace at the shoulders and the full half-sleeves. The color softened her ivory skin with its faint tinge of an excited blush and the sheen was reflected in her eyes.

She had been blessed with long, full lashes which could make her eyes look enormous when she was excited, and that they did now. Her high cheekbones complemented the upsweep of her hair and its coquettish tendrils perfectly, and her alabaster skin was her greatest asset. Annabelle had never thought of herself as pretty, and she did not now, but she thought the effect would do justice to Lucretia's reputation. As a finishing touch, she swept a filmy shawl through her elbows and tossed a final backward glance toward the glass. "Why," she thought in rising excitement, "I do look more like Lucy than I do myself!"

And with that confidence, she went to find her hostess.

The house was not large by the standards of country manors to which she was used; it was elegant and certainly spacious, but it was only a summer home and would not contain the winding corridors and myriad stairways one might expect in a permanent residence. So there was no excuse for Annabelle's getting lost, except that she had been too preoccupied with her own worries when being shown to her room to pay much heed to which direction the staircase lay.

After passing several closed doors and spying toward the end of the corridor what appeared to be a servants stairway, she ascertained she had made a wrong turn and proceeded to retrace her steps. It was then that she heard the voices issuing through a crack of a slightly open door which she was passing and, taking one of them for that of her hostess, she paused.

"I repeat, Devon, I am most disappointed in you." The female voice was high and huffy, and Annabelle knew then she should move on. "I dare swear this has been *the* most vexing day! Have you any idea how troublesome it is to prepare for a guest to arrive at luncheon and have her delayed until tea?"

The masculine voice which replied was mildly amused. "Surely you cannot blame me for that, auntie."

Annabelle's cheeks were burning. It was true, that eavesdroppers never heard good about themselves. Still, she had not intended to listen, only to find her hostess and, having found her, found the compulsion to linger very hard to resist. Especially since the gentleman with whom she was speaking was apparently the infamous Devon Lanson, the object of Lady Marbrough's matchmaking efforts, and most especially since they appeared to be discussing her.

"And neither did you do anything to relieve my distress, my fine sir! First not showing for luncheon at all—"

"Since the purpose of the invitation was to throw me into the arms of your latest designing heiress," he interrupted pleasantly, "I could say my arrival was perfectly timed. All's well that ends well, as they say."

"—and then to stroll in here in that get-up," continued Lady Marbrough heatedly.

"*Designing heiress!*" Annabelle thought, and drew herself up stiffly.

"Why," he replied innocently, "I thought I cut quite a dashing figure in my riding togs, and so did my stallion. Old clothes are best for riding," he informed her confidentially. "The horse grows familiar with the smell."

"Oh!" she replied in a strangulated tone. "You are disgusting!"

"I'm sorry to have disgusted you, auntie," he replied. His voice sounded closer to the door and Annabelle shrank back. "But don't you think we have kept the young lady waiting long enough?"

"Oh, Devon, sometimes I quite despair of you! If you are not going out of your way to dress like a buffoon or pretending to have left your manners in the gutter, you're dragging up from heaven-knows-where vulgar words like 'smell' into polite conversation . . ."

Now Annabelle had to clap her hand over her own mouth to smother laughter and she wondered how either of the conversationalists were keeping a straight face.

But he replied quite seriously, "I do beg your pardon! I was not aware . . . Would 'scent' perhaps be more appropriate? Or 'odor'? Or perhaps—"

"Oh, please, don't let's discuss it any further at all!"

Then, in a more restrained tone, "Why *do* you do this to me, Devon? After I go to such great lengths to build you up as a most desirable catch and the perfect gentleman I know you to be, you will always—*always*—make every effort to crush my dreams and fling them in my face! Why, it will soon get to the point that I cannot introduce you into polite society!"

"And what a pity that would be," he drawled.

"I have not yet recovered from the humiliation you dealt me last fall. Melissa Darnesbury's mother still is not speaking to me."

"Foolish chit," he replied carelessly. "Anyone who would make such a fuss over a spoilt gown is not worth my trouble."

"You spilled that punch on her deliberately," Lady Marbrough retorted. "Everyone says so! And then you proceeded to catch her train with your foot so that it ripped at the waist when she tried to get away. Oh, Devon, how could you?"

He was chuckling now. "Poor auntie. Why do you put yourself through such purgatory for me?"

"Because," she replied firmly, "you are my favorite relative."

"The connection is hardly so close to claim," he answered, his voice softening.

"Nonetheless, you are worth more than the whole lot of them packed together, and if it weren't for that bumbling barrister of mine, I would cheerfully cut them out to the penny and leave you my entire fortune."

"You know that is not possible," he answered gently. "And neither would I wish it."

"So the very least I can do is see you comfortably situated with a worthy bride."

"And you know that that is above all things precisely what I do not desire. When I marry, it will be of my own choosing and to a woman willing to live on *my* resources—meager though they may be."

"Please stop talking such romantic foolishness! Sometimes I think you have no earthly intention of marrying at all, but plan to grow old as solitary and discontented as that horrid old uncle you've taken such a fondness to."

"And sometimes I think that is not such an unpleasant fate."

"You know," Lady Marbrough pouted, "it is only because of my deep regard for you that I trouble myself at all. And I consider it highly ungrateful—"

"And you know," he interrupted smoothly, "that if it were not for my unquenchable affection for you I would not continue to accept your invitations and put myself through these blasted foolish paces to discourage your little ingenues. Really, auntie, I keep hoping you will one day take my hint."

"Oh! You are impossible!"

"As ever," he replied cheerfully. "And if there is nothing else, I am famished for tea and I rather imagine your guest is beginning to entertain quite a few notions of her own regarding *your* manners . . ."

"At least do something with that horrid cravat!"

"Oh, very well." His voice was very close now, and to her horror Annabelle saw the doorknob move. "I suppose I could attempt to straighten it . . ."

The door opened wider and she backed away quickly. "If you will allow me the use of one of your glasses . . ."

Turning quickly first this way and then the other, she fled into an empty bedchamber and closed the door quietly behind her just as the other door opened fully across the hall.

She took a few steps into the room and pressed her hands against her burning cheeks. What a horrid man! He had the audacity to refer to poor Lucretia as a "designing heiress" when it was so obviously he who was in need of making a successful match! Innocent, gullible Lucretia, whom he had never even met! Lucy, with her greatly exaggerated sense of delicacy, who would positively sink into the floor should her escort ever do anything so gauche as step on her gown or spill punch on it . . .

Annabelle had to stifle a giggle at the mental picture that produced. It would definitely make a chapter in her new book. The bumbling young buck of fashion who stumbles incorrigibly through the *ton* of London, dipping his lady's feathers in shrimp sauce and leaving a trail of muddy footprints and outraged mothers behind . . . She choked on laughter, but had to admit a grudging respect for any man who would go to such lengths to maintain his independence. It was only fortunate it was Annabelle with whom he would be dealing and not the impressionable and easily baffled Lucretia. She would only be careful in his presence to mind the train on her ball gown and learn to fetch her own punch . . .

The door opened suddenly and she whirled, and for a moment they only stared at one another.

He was a tall man, lean and muscularly framed. His skin was burnished with a healthy outdoor glow, in contrast to the sallow, wilting complexions most gentlemen of fashion held in such esteem. His face was stern and well molded, framed by a tousle of deep chestnut hair of an uncertain cut which looked as though he either enjoyed brisk rides in a high wind or was fond of constantly running his fingers through it. His brow was high, nose sharp and distinctive, and the cleft above the full lips was deep and somehow disconcerting . . . as though that mouth, once set into the stubborn lines it now formed, reflected a temperament not easily changed. The eyes were an intriguing shade of blue-green which at first reflected only surprise and then, as he swept her a sloppy bow, masked a faint contempt.

"Miss Arnsworth, I presume," he drawled. "How very charmed. I am Devon Lanson, at your service—or at least I will be in only a moment, as soon as I follow my aunt's instructions to make myself presentable for you."

He was dressed in a loose-fitting riding coat and breeches of rough homespun in a nondescript berry brown, scuffed boots, and a glaring yellow cravat which swung loosely about the open neck of his plain white shirt. It was, as her hostess had foretold, hardly the attire of one wishing to make an impression.

Without further ado and the utmost casualness, he strolled over to the pier glass and proceeded to tie his cravat.

She stammered, "I—I must have taken the wrong turn. I was on my way downstairs . . ."

"Of course." He turned with a flourish, putting the

finishing touches on a ridiculous Byronesque bow of his cravat, and gave her a charming smile. "There. That will do, don't you think?" As an afterthought, he glanced again at the glass, gave the bow a half turn so that it perched rakishly below his ear, and offered his arm. "I will be more than happy to show you the way, Miss Arnsworth. I can't tell you what a pleasure it is to make your acquaintance. I do believe we are going to get along famously."

She hoped he did not notice the stubborn set of her own jaw as she took his arm and then proceeded downstairs. Yes, indeed, it was most fortunate poor Lucy had not been cast at this man's mercy. He would find he had met his match in Annabelle Morgan.

CHAPTER 3

Annabelle could not know how neatly she had taken him by surprise, so quickly and smoothly had he hidden it. And the surprise was for more than simply finding an astonishingly pretty female in a room he had thought to be unoccupied, for the half-attentive reports he had heard of Lucretia Arnsworth had not prepared him for the woman of such inexplicable allure he had now discovered. He had expected her to be younger, for one thing. A silly, blushing debutante straight up from the country without a sound thought in her head. With this type of girl he was prepared to deal. He began to suspect uneasily it would not be quite so simple with this one, and worse, he was very much afraid he was beginning to lose some of the spirit of the game.

Annabelle was aware of the long, studious glances he fixed on her during tea and steeled herself to return them coolly. She thought once what a pity it was he was such a wretch, for in every other way he presented just the sort of man she might have liked to know better. She had very little time to spare for these reflections, however, because Lady Marbrough kept her thoughts quite well occupied elsewhere, and she was forced to keep her alertness at a peak to carry off this most important preliminary interview.

At first there was overwhelming relief that, for the moment, at least, she had not been discovered. Lady Marbrough was a thin, hawk-nosed woman with a back like a ramrod whose first action was to extend her hands to Annabelle and welcome her with a polite kiss on the cheek. Accustomed to her aunt's befuddled exuberance, Annabelle was amused by this woman's cool greeting and formal apology, very brief and correctly worded, for the delay. When Devon casually explained how they had met in the upper room, only a slight, uncontrollable quirk of the eyebrow betrayed her shock before the face resumed its placid, inscrutable lines, and she began to pour tea. Annabelle knew she had found another character for her book.

But she had to admire the woman's no-nonsense approach to the subject of her plans for her and Devon. "I know how difficult it will be for you to make new friends after being so long in seclusion," she explained matter-of-factly and passed Annabelle the delicately patterned cup of tea. "That is why I was so pleased Devon could find time to join us here for the summer. I am certain you will find you two have a great deal in common, and he will of course be available to take you around to all the *soirées* and musicales to which you will undoubtedly receive invitations."

Devon accepted his cup without expression before resuming his casual stance against the fireplace. "Indeed," he replied, "I am told I am quite a fine dancer. Do you dance, Miss Arnsworth?"

She assumed, in light of his apparent reputation for clumsiness, that he could not dance a step and she was on the point of retorting that her ball gowns had been acquired at too great an expense to be trampled on, but she smiled sweetly instead. "I am afraid I have been too long out of fashion to know the steps."

"Nonsense." Lady Marbrough brushed away the objection with an airy wave. "We are a very simple society here. The young people are still doing the same steps as did your mother, my dear."

"It would be most incorrect to do otherwise," murmured Devon.

Ignoring him, Lady Marbrough continued, "And how is your dear mother?"

Annabelle caught herself in a half-glance toward Devon, who kept himself deliberately out of her range of vision, and replied smoothly, "I am very much afraid she is losing her eyesight, madam, but she does not seem much concerned over it."

Lady Marbrough clicked her tongue in assumed sympathy. "You must persuade her to travel up to London. There is a very excellent gentleman there who makes the most miraculous spectacles, I am told."

"As you know," replied Annabelle, finding herself falling very easily into the role, "Mama does not like to travel much."

"And neither would I," put in Devon, "if I could not see where I was going."

Lady Marbrough shot him a warning glance, and Annabelle almost did not choke back an unexpected giggle quickly enough. She took a hasty sip of her tea.

"Do try some of these lovely cakes, Devon," insisted Lady Marbrough coolly.

"Thank you, I'd best not. I haven't washed."

Annabelle quickly glanced at Lady Marbrough and then away, pretending she had not heard. The poor woman looked as though she would sink with mortification, and Annabelle wondered with a brief stab of resentment what type of man could get such pleasure from torturing a convention-bound old lady.

"You see," he explained innocently to Annabelle, "it is a difficult habit to break. I spend most of my time working out of doors, and if I paused to wash each time my hands became soiled, there soon would be no time for anything else."

"Devon, please," urged Lady Marbrough a little desperately, "do eat something."

Annabelle lifted her chin pleasantly and said, "What type of work do you do, Mr. Lanson?"

For a moment he seemed taken aback. Clearly he had assumed that the mere revelation that her potential escort was a man who actually *worked*, would be enough to turn the spoiled Miss Arnsworth's head firmly away from him and toward a more delicate topic. Once again, Annabelle was grateful it was not Lucretia who sat in her place. Such an experience as Devon Lanson would be likely to turn her against society for the rest of her life.

Devon recovered himself smoothly and answered, "An uncle of mine has an estate in North Kent. It's not much of an estate, to be sure, and the poor old gentleman cannot afford a permanent overseer or in fact even a jack-of-all-trades about the place, so I fill that post for my keep."

In a nervous gesture reaching for the teapot, Lady Marbrough jarred the table and spilled tea all over the gleaming surface. "Oh, dear," she murmured, stabbing at the spill in distraction with a napkin. "How clumsy of me! Devon, do ring for Braddock."

"Here, let me help." He came quickly over to the table, jerked at the doily beneath the serving tray in an attempt to mop up the tea, and promptly sent teapot, cups, and sandwich tray tumbling onto the carpet.

"Oh my." He eyed the disaster with an admirable pretension of despair. "It seems clumsiness runs in the family, doesn't it?"

Annabelle stood, carefully guarding her own cup. With a great effort she bit back laughter and assured her hostess, "I am certain these things happen to everyone. Don't distress yourself, Lady Marbrough—at least nothing is broken. If you'll allow me, I will ring for the housekeeper and I am sure she will have everything put to rights in no time at all." As she spoke she crossed the room to tug at the bell cord, and when she turned with a smile she caught the surprised look in Devon's eyes just before he masked it. "In the meantime, what were we discussing?"

Lady Marbrough said weakly, "Thank you, my dear," and made a fidgeting gesture with the cameo at her puce-colored bodice, looking for all the world as though she wished to be anywhere else but in her own cozy parlor.

Devon said, rising to the occasion admirably, "My work on my uncle's estate. Are you interested in agriculture, Miss Arnsworth?"

"Of course not," put in Lady Marbrough, recovering sharply. "Lucretia is a well-bred young lady and knows nothing about crops and—animals, and such."

"Oh, but I am always anxious to learn," replied Annabelle sweetly. And, as an afterthought, she lifted her long lashes to him once, then dropped them down again and murmured, "I find gentlemen who work with their hands so exciting."

The confident light faded from his eyes, and the disturbed way his brows drew together could almost have been taken for a scowl, and Annabelle was jubilant. He said abruptly in a moment, "Do you indeed, Miss Arnsworth?" And then, regaining himself, "I say, there aren't many girls who would take it so rightly. Do you ride?"

"Oh, yes, indeed," replied Annabelle easily, though in fact she had no particular love for horses and her most lengthy jaunt had been to the village and back on a staid mare well past her prime.

"Famous!" he declared exuberantly. "You haven't ridden, Miss Arnsworth, until you've taken the beach at low tide. We'll make a party of it, shall we?"

"Devon," interrupted Lady Marbrough as Braddock entered in answer to the summons, "you know I dislike you riding on the beach. It is far too dangerous—and certainly unthinkable for a young lady . . . Oh, Braddock, we've had a little accident . . ."

With a disapproving glance at Devon, the housekeeper set about clearing away the mess. "Stains in the carpet," she muttered. "Never get 'em out."

"Oh, do whatever you think is best, Braddock," replied Lady Marbrough distractedly and rose to go over to Devon. "Surely, Devon, you can't be serious—"

"Oh, I am certain Miss Arnsworth is a fine horse-woman," he replied cheerfully. "And she will be in the most respectable of company. I will gather the party and we will make it near the first of July, shall we? We'll make a day of it and take a picnic luncheon. I do hope you are an early riser, Miss Arnsworth?"

"I am quite sure Lucretia will be far too exhausted with the balls and parties she will be attending," said Lady Marbrough firmly, "to consider rising at the crack of dawn for such a foolish adventure."

"On the contrary," put in Annabelle easily. "I shall look forward to it."

Devon bent a direct gaze upon her, and Annabelle felt her heart flutter unexpectedly in her chest. They were stern eyes, deep blue in their intensity, but she could not mistake a flicker of admiration there. They were not the eyes of a man she would have ordinarily liked to have lied to. She felt her courage beginning to sink and she had to bolster herself severely. She simply must not allow herself to weaken. There was far too much at stake here.

Braddock pushed by with the heavily laden tray and inquired dourly, "Shall I bring more tea, my lady?"

"Not on my account, I beg you," protested Devon. "I have left my horse quite long enough. I will be off to my rooms in town now to recuperate for the evening. Do we dine tonight, auntie?"

"Not tonight," replied Lady Marbrough with a severity which was only bordering on polite. "I feel certain Lucretia will be exhausted from her journey and would prefer to spend a quiet evening at home."

"Very well, then," he replied cheerfully and managed a short bow in Annabelle's direction. "I will call for you both tomorrow evening at nine. Until then?"

"Oh," put in Annabelle, "are we engaged for tomorrow?"

"And most every night this week. Unless," he added almost hopefully, "you have an objection?"

"I shall be looking forward to it," she replied sweetly and extended her hand with a little curtsey.

He hesitated for just the briefest moment and then took her fingers lightly between his strong brown ones. Annabelle could not explain the strange quivering in the pit of her stomach as he bent over her hand nor the unplanned fan of color to her cheeks which made her face look, for a moment, dazzling. Her confusion only increased as his eyes lingered on her face a moment longer than necessary and the expression there was no longer mocking. She was both relieved and sorry when he released her hand and straightened up, the familiar smooth mask covering his face and concealing what might have been revealed in his eyes. He turned to his aunt. "Thank you for the tea. And again, I am sorry if I—"

Lady Marbrough took his arm firmly. "I'll see you out, Devon."

In her distraction, she forgot to close the door behind her, and even though Annabelle quite properly resumed her seat at some distance from the doorway, she could not help overhearing the hushed voices which floated back inside.

"Oh, Devon, how *could* you?"

"I apologized for the spill, auntie, and there was nothing broken . . ."

"You know perfectly well that's not what I mean!" She made a strangled sound which suspiciously resembled a sob. "Oh, I did hope this time would be different!"

"Don't cry," he pleaded helplessly. "You know I did not intend to make your cry. I am truly sorry. It was not my intention to upset you, I vow it wasn't."

"I try so hard," she sniffled. "The least you could do is be polite."

"I will be polite," he promised quickly. "Only, please don't cry." A pause. "This young lady," he said in a moment thoughtfully, "is not like the others . . . and I cannot say now whether that is to the good or bad." Then, in a more normal tone, and with the resonance of firmness Annabelle remembered so well in the set of his mouth, "I promise to be polite, but nothing more. You must understand, auntie, however dearly I hold you, I will lead my own life."

Again Lady Marbrough sniffed, but her voice had regained its calm tenor. "You will not be late tomorrow," she enjoined him, "and neither will you come dressed in some outrageous costume . . ."

"I will be polite," he reiterated, and the door opened on a cheerful "À *bientôt!*"

Annabelle juggled the empty teacup from one hand to the other, feeling uncomfortable despite her own firm self-assurances that she had no reason to be so. She had stumbled into an awkward situation, but all was not as desperate as it appeared. On the one hand, her promise to Lucretia would be much easier to keep since the gentleman with whom she was dealing was just as anxious to discourage her as she was to be rid of him. On the other hand, her instincts rebelled at his harsh prejudgment of her, alias Lucretia, and it was her intention—indeed, her duty—to teach him a lesson he would not soon forget.

In the meantime, she must be very careful to remember that the entire purpose of this little plot had been to discourage him, and as she watched from the open window his glossy black stallion dash by in a spatter of turf, she was not feeling very cheerful.

Lady Marbrough came back in, her face composed into its usual placid lines, no signs of the distress she had displayed for Devon's benefit now visible. She arranged the folds of her rustling silk gown about her in the chair across from Annabelle, folded her hands, and began pleasantly, "I do hope you will not allow my nephew's sense of humor to distract you. He has a streak of boyishness about him and is fond of playing rather unamusing games."

Annabelle said politely, "He is quite charming, I am sure. And it will be a comfort to have a member of the family, as it were, to take me about. How thoughtful of you to have arranged it."

"Quite right, my dear," her hostess replied firmly. "I hold my duty to your mother much too highly to allow you to fall in with anyone whom I did not trust implicitly. My Devon," she continued confidentially, "is not a man of great fortune, but I can assure you of his very fine character. And of course, I've no need to dwell upon the quality of his family . . ." She gave a small self-deprecating smile which Annabelle acknowledged with a nod. "He is not, in direct line of descent, my nephew, of course, but my late husband thought very highly of his father, who was a younger son of no means and the second husband of my cousin Elvira who was widowed of Lord Simmington shortly after the birth of his heir. Of course Devon was orphaned quite young, after the terrible coach accident which took both his parents, but still, all might have come to rights for him had not his half-brother, the present Lord Simmington, squandered his fortune even to the point of losing the family hall . . . a most distressing business, I can assure you. It came about then that Devon was shipped off to live with his father's brother in North Kent and Lord Simmington . . . well, I'm sure one doesn't hear much of him these days. I believe he might be recuperating on the Continent somewhere. It is all a quite tragic story which I am sure you have heard often enough."

Indeed, thought Annabelle, she had. The only dissimilarity in their stories was that Annabelle had been fortunate to be taken in by kind and generous kin upon whom her presence put no burden. She encouraged, "Do go on."

"I cannot but find it admirable," Lady Marbrough continued a little dubiously, "that he displays such devotion to his impoverished uncle and to that great monster of a house he claims, though perhaps in that case he does not exercise as much judgment as I would like. The old gentleman is quite eccentric," she confided, "and I suspect he is not quite a good influence on the boy." Annabelle had to smother a smile at the reference to the mature young gentleman she had just met as a "boy."

"At any rate," Lady Marbrough added with a frown, "he cannot have Devon's best interest at heart, for he uses him terribly and at no expectation of recompense."

"Surely," said Annabelle, "Mr. Lanson is aware that he can expect nothing from his uncle?"

Lady Marbrough nodded sadly. "Which is where he shows a sad lack of concern over his future, which is his only failing."

"I think," replied Annabelle without meaning to, "that it is quite refreshing in this day and age to discover someone willing to help another without expecting anything in return."

Lady Marbrough smiled, pleased. "I knew I could be frank with you, my dear. What a joy you must be to your mother!"

Annabelle lowered her eyes and tried to blush girlishly. She found it easier than she had expected, for she was discovering she did not like to deceive anyone, not even for a cause as noble as this one.

"Now," continued Lady Marbrough enthusiastically, "I want you to enjoy yourself to the fullest while you are here. I have always thought it the gravest of errors for your mother to have kept you locked away with her for such a time. But no mind now, because you are here and all that is to be corrected. You will be meeting a great many young people—we will be at home tomorrow afternoon and I expect quite a stream of callers—and you must feel free to accept any invitations you care to. Tomorrow night we are engaged for the Wesley *soirée*. We will give a quiet evening for a select number of friends on Wednesday, and, oh my, at the beginning of the season there are so many invitations I can scarce keep up with them!"

"Perhaps you will allow me to relieve you of that duty," suggested Annabelle. "At home I often help my au— My mother," she corrected quickly, "with her correspondence."

Lady Marbrough beamed. "What a charming child you are! I can see now I was quite mistaken to fret about your welfare, for the years of deprivation can only have sweetened your temper."

"Thank you, Lady Marbrough," replied Annabelle. "But I cannot say I have felt at all deprived."

Lady Marbrough reached forward to pat Annabelle's hand briefly. "You will only now begin to see what you have missed." She rose with a swish of skirts and the soft scent of lavender, and Annabelle rose too. "Now, I have been thoughtless of your fatigue quite long enough. You go upstairs and refresh yourself, and I believe I will do the same. We dine at eight."

"Thank you," Annabelle answered. "I would enjoy an opportunity to nap, and I believe I will begin a letter." At the door she turned. "Thank you for having me, Lady Marbrough."

The older woman smiled confidently. "Believe me when I tell you, my dear, the pleasure is entirely mine."

In Annabelle's leather writing case, a gift from Lucy many Christmases past, was an inkstand, quill, sealing wax, and delicately initialed stationery. Also, in more abundant supply, was a stack of plain, unmarked manuscript paper, and Annabelle debated for a moment which kind of paper to take up first. There were so many impressions of the adventure she wanted to get down in writing, for the possibilities for her new book were so vivid they positively made her fingers tingle. But Lucretia, giddy with daydreams of her Freddy and probably fraught with anxiety over Annabelle, was likely to become so befuddled that she would blurt out everything to her mother if she did not hear from Annabelle soon. At any rate, Annabelle was in no mood to rest, so she reluctantly took out a sheet of stationery and sat down.

Dipping her quill into the ink, her eye caught the trailing scrollwork of initials and she scowled. "APM." Annabelle Penelope Morgan. That could present a problem. As well as could the difficulty of posting a letter addressed to "Lucretia Catherine Arnsworth," but it was positively vital that they keep in communication.

Quickly, she dashed off:

"Dearest Lucy—Please remember to address your reply to this letter to 'Lucretia Arnsworth' and do not, I pray you, allow it to fall into any hands other than your own. The utmost care must be exercised in posting it, for you would look most silly should you be discovered attempting to post a letter addressed to yourself . . ."

She sat back, gathering her thoughts, hoping that Lucy would not be too scatterbrained to heed her advice. Then she continued:

"So far you will be pleased to know we are undiscovered in our deception, which is a matter which caused me some concern from the moment I arrived here. There were so many details, Lucy, we overlooked that I am quite amazed I ever could have been so foolish as to agree to this plan! But do not be concerned —all, I believe, will come to the best, and, as for my part, I am growing more confident with each moment that we have done the right thing. You would have walked into a situation more awkward than you first imagined had you come in my stead, but more of that later.

"Lady Marbrough is a kind hostess, but very amusing in her obsession with all that is proper. I think you would have gotten along with her very well. I endeared myself to her immediately by being pleasant to her nephew, who is the light of her life, and who is, of course, quite another story altogether."

Here she paused, puzzling over how to continue. How could she put on paper the strange fascination of this man of paradoxes, the strength in his blue-green eyes and the touch of his fingers, the windblown hair and sun-honeyed skin and the rough, determined face . . . the man whom the two young women had intended to victimize and who, it was becoming more dangerously apparent by the moment, was far more likely to do the same to Annabelle. She should describe him as crude and cruel and selfish, but a sense of fairness would not allow her to be so explicit. She wrote merely:

"An interesting development has occurred with Devon Lanson. It appears that Lady Marbrough has been attempting to make a match for him for years and he will have nothing to do with it. He, in fact, goes out of his way to discourage any hopeful his aunt presents to him and I—alias you—am no exception. I almost could return home now with a job well done but for the fact that we are in it this far, and," she had to add honestly, "I find myself taking strong exception to the way in which he so arrogantly abuses the good intentions of his aunt and tramples upon the sensibilities of unsuspecting young girls and, as I am already here, intend to give him a lesson or two in manners.

"Dearest Lucy, I know this must be terribly confusing to you and that you had much rather hear of all the sights and sounds and the latest fashions I have encountered since my arrival, and I promise to write more on this note later. I merely wanted to assure you of my safe arrival and the success of what I must reluctantly refer to as our 'fraud' . . . I understand there are scores of invitations already to balls and galas and I promise my next letter will be much more colorful. In the meantime, do give my love to your mother, and to you, my fervent hopes that all will come right with Freddy.

"I remain your most affectionate cousin, Annabelle."

And, in a bold underline, "*P.S. Please do not forget to take the utmost care in posting your reply!*"

Carefully she sealed the letter and scrawled the fateful address, then hid it well in the bottom of her writing case. Then she took out a fresh sheet of paper and happily wrote the first words of the sixth chapter of her newest novel, "He was a most extraordinary man . . ."

CHAPTER 4

Lady Marbrough did not exaggerate when she predicted a veritable "stream" of callers between two and five the next afternoon. They came singly, in couples, by threes and fours, mamas and daughters, great-aunts and uncles, a few bold young men escorting their sisters or mothers, all anxious to have a look at the heretofore undiscovered young heiress Lady Marbrough had chosen to spring upon them without much more than a moment's notice, in a manner, they all went away agreeing, which was annoyingly typical of her.

Annabelle dressed in a becoming rose silk frock embroidered in deeper pink buds and stems and knew that the shade complimented her own coloring extravagantly. She arranged her hair below her left ear in a single knot of curls which dangled enchantingly when she laughed. And while making these elaborate preparations with her toilette, she sternly denied to herself that the effort was all in the hope that Devon Lanson would stop by.

But as the hours wore on toward five o'clock it became obvious that he did not consider the making of formal calls in keeping with his role. Annabelle sat primly in the stiff-backed chair until her feet began to tingle, she accepted gallant compliments with a shy deference of which her hostess noddingly approved, she engaged old gentlemen and staid matrons in the type of harmless chatter at which she had become adept in her aunt's household, and she knew she was making a fine impression. She was also so bored she could have screamed.

After a nearly disastrous morning, her nerves were on edge and she was in no mood to attempt to occupy her thoughts with absurd tea-table chatter while her real concerns lay elsewhere. More and more with each passing moment she began to suspect the risky charade had no hope of working.

She had been anxious to post her letter to Lucy the very first thing, and Lady Marbrough insisted upon hitching up the carriage and accompanying her the five or so blocks to the post office. Earnestly, Annabelle pleaded with her not to bother, but Lady Marbrough replied casually, "The morning air will refresh us both. Besides, I found time last evening to dash off a note to your mother. I'm anxious to send it on its way."

Annabelle's heart sank. At least she could be grateful her aunt would not read Lady Marbrough's letter save through Lucy's careful interpretation. She only hoped her cousin had the presence of mind to scan the missive first for references to "your lovely daughter" and "your dear Lucretia" before reading out loud to her mother. And then another horrible thought occurred: Suppose Lucy, flibbertigibbet-minded as she was, allowed the duty of reading her mother's mail to fall on other shoulders—a servant's, perhaps, or a well-meaning friend? What disasters that would unfold!

So preoccupied was she with those thoughts which were threatening to pull her deeper and deeper into morbidity that she quite forgot the problem posting her own letter might produce. It was when the postmaster, after chatting politely with Lady Marbrough for a few minutes, turned to her and smiled, "Miss Arnsworth? Did you have something for me today?" that she realized her hand, inside her reticule, clutched an incriminating paper addressed to "Miss Lucretia Arnsworth." She let it drop back as though it were a hot thing.

"Oh dear," she exclaimed, flustered. "Silly me! After all this fuss and I have left it on my dressing table! What a perfect dolt I am!"

"Never mind, my dear," Lady Marbrough comforted. "We will have one of the girls take it by later. At least your mother will have *my* letter to assure her of your safe arrival. Now I am in great need of a skein of blue silk to complete my needlework etching . . ."

And so they went in search of blue thread, and by the time they returned home Annabelle could think of only one solution to the letter-writing problem. She must address her letters to Lady Arnsworth or to Annabelle Morgan and only hope that Lucretia had the presence of mind to read them herself first.

As the afternoon shadows lengthened and the march of callers grew thinner, Annabelle's disappointment became keener. The one thing which might have relieved the tedium of this dreadful day would have been Devon's presence. If only he would swagger in, break a few things, insult one or two of the fat old cows who were scrutinizing her from behind gold-rimmed lorgnettes, and then tumble out as gracefully as he had entered, the endless hours of sitting in this cramped position and filling the room with inane chatter might be worth it.

But instead she found herself trying to keep her eyes off the little French ormolu clock on the mantel and attempting to hold a conversation with an empty-headed young lady by the name of Caroline Beckett.

"Oh, yes indeed," Caroline was saying airily, "you must come to our little at-home a week from Saturday night. A very *small* gathering, you understand, but for myself I find simplicity quite refreshing after the positively *hectic* London season . . . although I daresay this must seem to you the very height of adventure after being so long shut away." She gave her blonde curls a negligent toss. "I do mean to say, a proper mourning is one thing, but I find it the height of cruelty to lock a young lady away just at the very *peak* of her career . . . My dear, it must have been awful!"

Annabelle smiled noncommittally. "I am of course very grateful to Lady Marbrough for this invitation."

Caroline giggled and cast a covert glance in the direction of Lady Marbrough, who was engaged in an engrossing conversation with two other matrons about a third, who was not present. Caroline drew her sweetly perfumed head closer to Annabelle's confidentially and added in a hushed tone, "Whatever you do, do *not* allow her to draw you into an alliance with that dreadful relative of hers. I understand he is in town and, really, she has tried to pawn him off on every marriageable young lady with a penny in her stocking since time began!"

Annabelle lifted an eyebrow coolly and replied, "Oh, really?"

"Yes, indeed," continued Caroline enthusiastically, still careful to keep a wary eye on the group across the room and to maintain a conspiratorial tone. "It is the most disgraceful thing. He hasn't a farthing to his name, you know, and keeps himself hidden away in Kent somewhere on a dreary estate which does not even belong to him and for which he has no expectations and which, I understand, is positively crumbling to the ground! I have not met him, which I suppose is all to my good fortune, but I understand he has the manners of a buffoon, and she insists upon repeatedly dragging him into society like an unbroken puppy she is trying to pass off as a lapdog! Why, I have heard some tales . . ."

Annabelle, keeping rein on her temper with great difficulty, discovered at that moment the perfect distraction, as her hostess, rising to greet a gentleman who had just entered the room, beckoned to her. "Excuse me," she said, with a stiff smile. "I must go greet our visitor."

"Oh, that's just Bertie," giggled Caroline. "Only he would be bold enough to come alone and just to get a look at you. You have set the entire town on its ear," she confided as Annabelle tried to pull away, "and no doubt Bertie has been selected as a committee of one to report back on you to the other young gentlemen before the *soirée* tonight."

Trying very hard not to scowl, Annabelle went over to her hostess.

"Lucretia," said Lady Marbrough, "may I present

Bertram Dosset? Bertram, may I present the daughter of a very dear friend, Miss Lucretia Arnsworth?"

There might have at once been a flicker of some surprise in Bertie's eyes, but other than that, no expression to warn her of what was to come. He was the very picture of a fashionable young-man-about-town, in a smooth gray jacket and conservatively striped waistcoat, the collar so high and stiff it met the edges of his sideburns at the precise angle they curved toward his chin and the spotless cravat impeccably tied. His profile was regular and well bred, the thin lips etched into just the faintest trace of an aristocratic sneer, and perhaps it was a hint of steel in those scrutinizing eyes which Annabelle, a born observer of character, noticed. Perhaps it was simply the way he examined her, only a moment longer than was strictly polite, which made her uncomfortable.

Then he turned to Lady Marbrough and said the fatal words, "But how unfair of you, ma'am. You gave me no warning it was the lovely Miss Arnsworth who was to be your houseguest. You see, we have already met."

Annabelle's heart literally leaped to her throat, so that she could not speak, nor hardly even breathe. He took her hand and bent over it, hiding what she suspected was a knowing smile. "I never dreamt to have an opportunity to renew our acquaintance so soon, as I get out to the country so rarely and I had heard you do not travel to London. How very delighted I am that our paths have crossed again."

Lady Marbrough said pleasantly, "How fortunate for

you, my dear, to find yourself not completely among strangers."

Annabelle managed, "Yes, indeed . . . ," and she was thinking frantically, How can this be? When could he have met Lucy without my knowing?

He lifted his head and his eyes were dancing with unpleasant mirth. "Ah, but I am stricken! I can tell Miss Arnsworth does not recall the occasion of our last encounter, which was, I assure you, one of the most memorable events of my life." He tucked her arm confidently through his and turned to Lady Marbrough. "Please excuse us, ma'am, while I attempt to refresh Miss Arnsworth's memory or return to my humble abode with shattered sensibilities. It was at Farrington Hall," he continued while Annabelle's mind was racing frantically. "I was with my cousin Lowrey Knox, with whom I was stopping on my way to London. We had tea together and quite a nice chat. Pray, Miss Arnsworth, do not be cruel! It was scarce a month ago and you cannot have forgotten so soon!"

Farrington Hall was an estate ten miles to the west of Arnsworth Hall. Lucretia and her mother frequently visited there, but not as frequently as did Lowrey Knox, who was enraptured with the youngest daughter of the house but too shy to come to the point. And this man, his cousin!

She said quite equably, withdrawing her arm as he returned her to her seat beside Caroline, "Of course I recall the occasion, Mr. Dosset. I was merely somewhat taken aback by your own excellent memory. I should not have thought a gentleman such as you, with so wide a circle of friends, would remember one meeting with a simple country girl."

Her heart was thudding in her bosom to the rhythm of "a month ago"! He would have to be either myopic or stupid to fail to remark the difference between that Lucretia and the present one, and her instincts told her strongly he was neither.

"Why, Bertie!" accused Caroline coquettishly. "You have had the edge on us all and you have kept it secret, you wretch! Why did you not mention you were acquainted with Miss Arnsworth when all the town has been buzzing to meet her?"

He drew up a hassock at their feet and sparked Annabelle a wicked glance. "Why," he replied smoothly, "I was not until this moment aware that the charming young lady to whom I was introduced at Farrington Hall and Lady Marbrough's summer guest were one and the same. But it is a happy coincidence—for us both, I hope," he added innocently, and Annabelle had to swallow hard as she felt an almost strangulating heat swimming to her cheeks.

He *did* know, she was certain of it. That maddening gleam of laughter in his eyes confirmed it whenever she chanced to glance his way. But, she argued with herself not very hopefully, if he were certain, why did he not expose her now and have done with it? Perhaps there was a chance, after all.

"And how is your mother?" he was saying pleasantly. "Your mother and mine were great friends before Lady Arnsworth retired to the country, you may recall. She was most pleased to hear we had come upon one another and I believe intended to renew a correspondence with your mother. I can just think how delighted both our parents will be to hear we have met again in Brighton."

"Indeed," managed Annabelle, and tried not to imagine a threat in his words. Fie on Lucy and her simpleminded schemes! What kind of tangle had Lucy gotten them into now, and how would Annabelle ever come out of it?

"And my cousin Lowrey?" he continued, still holding her with those nastily gleaming eyes. "Have you seen him since we last met? I am quite remiss at family obligations, I fear, and often am the last for any news. I am thinking," he added meaningfully, "however, of mending my ways."

"Actually," replied Annabelle, "I have not been about much . . ."

"Well, we shall mend all that, now that you are here," Bertie announced decisively. "I am planning a reception at the end of August which will be the most unusual event of the season, and of course you will be there."

"Oh, what fun!" exclaimed Caroline. "Bertie does give the most original parties. Do tell us more!"

"Ah, but this will be quite unlike anything *you* have ever attended, dear Caro," Bertram assured her and passed a sly half-smile to Annabelle. "Miss Arnsworth has herself only this moment inspired me."

"Well, of all the peculiar things," replied Caroline with a little pout. "What can be so inspiring about a reception in Brighton?"

"It is a secret," he told her with a disturbing twinkle

in his eye. And then he turned to Annabelle, "Do you like secrets, Miss Arnsworth?"

He knew. There was no doubt about it. Her courage seemed to be lost somewhere in the pit of her stomach, but she managed to reply coolly, "As long as they are in good taste, Mr. Dosset."

He smiled, apparently satisfied, and stood. "Well, I must be off. I will see you at the Wesley affair tonight, Miss Arnsworth, will I not?"

She rose a little shakily. "I will be there."

Again, the insinuating smile as he bent over her hand. "Do reserve a dance for me. We have so much to talk about." He bowed briefly to Caroline and then crossed the room to make his adieus to the other ladies.

"That Bertie," muttered Caroline discontentedly when he was gone. "He is so full of himself, and a terrible flirt. He will be the Marquis of Dunnore one day, you know, which is quite a respectable title, but, still, I understand his family is not quite as solvent as it once was. Mama says it is high time he stopped gaming about and set his sights on a good match, if he intends to save the family fortune." But her eyes, as she watched Bertram leave the room, quite aside from the petulance in her tone, were those of a young woman with injured vanity. Annabelle realized abruptly that Caroline was perhaps hoping that match would be made with herself.

Of all imaginable, wretched turns of events, thought Annabelle despairingly as the last of their late afternoon callers departed, this was by and far the worst. Certainly the only thing to do was to make a clean breast of it to Lady Marbrough and return home immediately. It had been foolishness from the start and in only a day had landed Lucretia and herself in more hot water than all of Annabelle's cunning and care could possibly rescue them from.

But then there was Lucy. Annabelle had entered into a bargain with her, thoughtlessly and carelessly perhaps, but it was a bargain nonetheless. What would become of Lucretia if word of this ever got out? Far worse than the wrath of her mother, there was Lucretia's reputation to be considered and she on the very verge of bringing poor Freddy to the sticking point! Her hopes of marital bliss would be dashed and she would perhaps forever be resigned to spinsterhood, all because of one rash and carefree little deception.

"Lucretia, my dear," said Lady Marbrough with some concern. "You look a little peaked. I hope you are not unwell?"

Annabelle passed a hand over her brow distractedly. "Perhaps a bit too much excitement."

"Then you must go upstairs and rest immediately. We cannot miss the Wesley *soirée* tonight, when already you have made such a sensation."

Not half the sensation I will make, thought Annabelle grimly, as she climbed the stairs to her room, should my worst expectations become fact . . .

Inside her room she locked the door and went immediately to her writing case, rummaging about for the unposted letter. Unsealing it, she added a desperate postscript in the margin: "Lucy—write immediately. Do you recall meeting last month at Farrington Hall a perfectly dreadful man by the name of *Bertram Dosset?*"

Once again she sealed the letter and hid it safely. She wandered over to the bed and lay down, but was too troubled to sleep. Her mind was filled with macabre thoughts of the surprises Bertram Dosset would be planning for their next encounter.

CHAPTER 5

Somehow the precious rose ball gown did not seem quite fitting to Annabelle's mood that evening, and when she heard Devon's voice in the lower hall she was putting the finishing touches on the spring-green ensemble which promised all the frivolity of a young girl intent upon a gay evening. In her ears she clasped a pair of Lucretia's pearl earrings, and about her throat was the matching necklace fastened with a cluster of diamonds. She paused before the glass for one last appraising look, and the chambermaid who had helped her dress breathed softly, "Ye look lovely, miss, that ye do."

The *décolletage* of shimmering material pushed her breasts high and round, and into this she carefully inserted the flat "bosom vase" which held a single, deep pink rosebud. Its vibrant color seemed to spread its blush over her shoulders and neck to highlight her cheekbones and dance in her eyes. The color was in fact the result of the excitement of a challenge, for some time between a light dinner and the beginning of the arduous dressing process she had come to realize that if she could beat Devon at his own game, she could do the same to the impudent Mr. Dosset. And she was tingling with impatience to begin.

From the bodice the gown fell to accent her slender

waist and flat abdomen, then gathered in the back with
rows of ruching and lace, just covering her ankles with a
swirl of fine pleats and scallops of white netting. Her
velvet slippers, another extravagant gift from the generous Lucretia, were emerald colored and fastened with
tiny gold buckles. "Why," thought Annabelle in amazement and delight as she appreciated her reflection a moment longer, "I feel like Cinderella!"

She pulled on her gloves and snatched up her ivory-
handled fan, pausing a moment as the maid arranged a
white net shawl about her shoulders, and descended the
stairs.

Devon was chatting with his aunt in the receiving
parlor, and he rose when Annabelle came in. He was
correctly dressed in evening attire, perfect in every detail from the dove-gray waistcoat to the spotless white
lace at his sleeve to the polished Hessians, and relief at
this fact showed on Lady Marbrough's face. But it was
Devon's face with which Annabelle was concerned at
the moment. Something in her chest tightened uncontrollably as she saw those stern features soften and the
brief flicker of admiration light his eyes as he looked at
her. And he said, "A very good evening to you, Miss
Arnsworth."

She made a small curtsey and felt her natural color
heighten as his eyes took in every detail of her appearance in a leisurely and appreciative fashion, from the
dancing earrings which shadowed the curve of her jaw
to the tips of her velvet slippers and at last came to rest
on the little rosebud at her bosom.

"I see we are of a like mind," he said in a moment,

and there was a strange tone to his voice which she did not recognize from the afternoon before. It was gentler, more refined, and when he came toward her she felt that uncomfortable and uncontrollable fluttering in her chest begin again.

He presented her with a small nosegay of rosebuds in the exact same hue as the one she wore, and, accepting them, she said lightly, "Perhaps it is only that we have the same florist, Mr. Lanson."

Immediately the stern mask came over his features again, and just as immediately she regretted the flippant reply. She added quickly, "They are lovely. Thank you."

He nodded briefly and turned to his aunt. "I believe I heard Nob bring the carriage around. Shall we go?"

He offered his arm to Lady Marbrough and, almost as an afterthought, to Annabelle. Annabelle felt bereft. "You are being as silly as Lucy," she told herself sternly as the footman assisted her into the carriage. "The purpose, after all, was to discourage him . . ." And it was her own fault if she had allowed the process to become more painful than she had planned.

In the brief ride to the Wesley home, Devon sat casually across from them while Lady Marbrough chatted about the people they were to meet and the favorable impression Annabelle had already made. The changing shadows which the street lamps and carriage lamps played on Devon's face caused Annabelle to imagine perhaps more moodiness than was actually there, and she found herself wondering uneasily what diabolical schemes he was plotting for this evening. To remove her thoughts from this depressing course and steer the conversation away from herself, she said brightly, "That gentleman I met this afternoon—Mr. Dosset?—remarked that he was planning an affair in August which would take the town quite by surprise. He made quite a fuss of it, and I must admit it sounded quite exciting. Whatever do you suppose it could be?"

There was a brief silence, and Annabelle thought Devon's position, from deep within the carriage, grew more alert. But it was his aunt who spoke. "Oh dear," she sighed. "I meant to warn you about him, my dear. It is not that he is not from one of the very finest families and holds a noble name—why, his father and my dear late husband were known to ride to hounds together every season for fifteen years—but there are certain things—that is to say, his reputation is not perhaps quite what it should be . . ."

"What my aunt is so delicately trying to say," put in Devon abruptly, "is that you would do well to put as much distance between yourself and Bertram Dosset as possible, as would any young lady who has grown fond of her reputation the way it is."

Lady Marbrough laughed a little nervously. "Really, Devon, I hardly think we need be that harsh . . ."

"With all due respect, auntie," answered Devon curtly, "there are things about this—gentleman"—he seemed to wrestle with the word—"which I suspect even you do not know. Miss Arnsworth would do well to heed my advice."

"It isn't that he is not *received*," replied Lady Marbrough a little petulantly, as though she realized her nephew's tone brooked no contradiction but was persuaded by her own position to try. "And if he intends to send us an invitation to his little gathering, we cannot very well refuse without seeming to cut him, and for no good reason . . ."

"He seemed quite charming to me," put in Annabelle innocently, burning with curiosity to learn more about this man whom she suspected was well on his way to becoming her archenemy. "What can he have done that is so terrible we must cut him?"

Devon fastened her with those penetrating eyes for an uncomfortable moment. "That is, I beg leave to say, of no consequence to you," he told her, "nor to any young lady of breeding. I merely feel it my duty to urge you as strongly as I can to walk carefully where Mr. Dosset is concerned."

"And if you should receive an invitation," she pursued, frustrated. "Will you go?"

He lifted his shoulders negligently. "I hardly think the question is material, as I doubt very much I will be in Brighton when the event occurs."

Lady Marbrough looked at him in dismay. "But Devon, you promised me the summer!"

"I am sorry, aunt," he replied, "but my uncle is in failing health, as I believe I told you, and I cannot but feel uneasy at leaving him so long."

The carriage pulled up before the gaily lit house and Devon smothered Lady Marbrough's further protests by smiling sweetly and insisting, "Come now, don't let us argue and spoil Miss Arnsworth's evening! Eat, drink, and be merry, for tomorrow is soon enough to be at one another's throats again."

As Annabelle walked up the steps with Devon's hand lightly on her elbow, it was easy to allow all thoughts but appreciation for the present to flee from her mind. Colored lanterns lit the walkway and swung gently in shades of pink and blue and gold over the open door, and the cloying scent of gardenia was wafted over the night air. Inside there must have been a thousand candles on the walls, mirrored in chandeliers, winking off the ladies' jewels, and reflected from gilt-framed ovals of glass. The hall was filled with vases of fresh flowers, tall-stemmed gladioli, spidery birds-of-paradise, clusters of passion-pink peonies and blood-red roses. The walls were trimmed with swags of greenery and studded with clusters of waxy white gardenias which dripped their fragrant scent over the festivities below and mixed headily with the aroma of burning wax and other blossoms and the ladies' perfumes. So passionately had Annabelle researched this very scene for her book, so avidly had she drunk up every word of gossip from the visitors to her aunt's home, that she should have felt right at home stepping out of the pages of a manuscript and into the reality. Instead, she found herself experiencing a strong urge to pinch herself to make certain she was not dreaming.

In the reception line were her host and hostess, their daughter and two sons and a daughter-in-law, and Annabelle floated through it as on air, making no effort to remember names or faces, her senses filled with the sights and sounds of all around her. Lady Marbrough dragged her off to introduce her to several matrons of her acquaintance and their daughters, and again Annabelle allowed the names to slip by her. Then, in a typically frank manner which Annabelle was learning to admire, Lady Marbrough gave them a dismissing wave and sank to the satin-covered divan beside her friends. "I will leave Lucretia's welfare in your most capable hands, Devon," she said. "You young people go along and have a good time."

"Take care, ma'am," Devon murmured, bowing to her, "that your trust is not misplaced." Annabelle knew that the moment he had put on his other face and she missed poignantly the unpretentious young man who had greeted her at Lady Marbrough's home less than an hour ago.

In a corner a string quartet was screened by flowery summer foliage, and several couples were engaged in the staid steps of a court dance. From another room a door opened onto a gleaming buffet table, and it was in this direction Devon guided her. "It must be the heat at these affairs," he commented as he placed his hand lightly upon her arm, "which makes a man uncommonly thirsty. Will you join me in a glass of punch?"

The mention of the word "punch" brought back the memory of the overheard conversation the day before and had its inevitable affect on her. She clamped her lips together primly on a bubble of laughter. But she could not resist replying, "I trust you do not mean that literally, sir."

He glanced at her and surprised her with a quirk of his eyebrow which might have been a struggle against his own laughter. But again the blank mask came down as he continued politely, "I hope you will not find all this frivolity too tedious. I am certain it is quite unlike anything you are used to."

"No, indeed," she replied enthusiastically, "I find it all very exciting."

He looked at her with some surprise as he accepted two glasses of punch from a nearby servant. "Is that true?" he commented mildly. "I would have thought otherwise."

"Do I take that to mean," she replied conversationally, "that you do find these affairs tedious?"

His eyes scanned the room as though looking for some way to escape. "Dreadfully."

"They why do you attend them?" she demanded pleasantly.

Still he avoided her eyes. "It seems to please my aunt. I am rather fond of her and do occasionally exert myself to please her."

"Well, you certainly have a strange way of showing it," she retorted, unable to contain herself any longer. "You cannot but be aware that your little pranks cause her great distress and extreme mortification, and yet you persist without pity or shame. It is a great wonder to me that she continues to tolerate you."

Now he looked at her, and his lips curved into a slight smile of acknowledgment. "I see my reputation has preceded me. But you, Miss Arnsworth, should perhaps take greater care over your tongue, lest you become known as forward."

She lifted her chin defiantly. "It is a habit acquired too early in life to break now, and I see no point in trying. I am quite used to speaking my mind on any subject which disturbs me."

He examined her with a strange and searching look. "And do I disturb you so?"

She had to lower her eyes, growing uncomfortable under his gaze. "Indeed yes," she answered. "That is, I find your treatment of your aunt most distasteful and extremely disturbing . . ."

He turned back to his glass of punch negligently. "My aunt is a dear creature," he replied, "but unfortunately inclined to meddle in affairs which do not concern her. And it is no more my fault than hers that I find myself more comfortable riding the acres or tending a sick sheep than on a ballroom floor, nor that my fortune is fixed and shows every likelihood of remaining so. It is to her best interest to learn to accept the facts as they are."

This last was issued as a challenge, and as much as Annabelle would have loved a chance to reply, she was prevented from doing so by a cheerful hail from across the room.

"Lucretia! *Dear* Lucretia!"

It was Caroline Beckett, approaching with the enthusiasm which declared it might have been years instead of mere hours since they had last met and dragging with her a rather awkward young gentleman she tightly clutched by the arm. "Oh, how glad I am to have spotted you," she exclaimed, clasping both her hands and presenting her cheek for a kiss. "And whatever can you be thinking, hiding away here when all the fun is out there?" Before Annabelle could reply, Caroline quickly brought forward the young man. "May I present my brother Arnold, who has been absolutely *famished* to meet you. Arnold, this is my very dear friend Lucretia Arnsworth."

The young man blinked rapidly, recovered himself, and made his bow. "Charmed, I'm sure, Miss Arnsworth."

As Caroline was staring quite pointedly at Devon, Annabelle was forced to introduce him. She began to suspect that was the point in Caroline's coming over at all, and considering the unsavory things Caroline had said about him only that afternoon, Annabelle found that strange.

"How delightful, Mr. Lanson," murmured Caroline, extending her hand, over which he properly bowed. "Lady Marbrough has spoken of you so often. I can't think how we've failed to meet before."

"I believe the solution to that puzzle is quite simple," replied Devon smoothly, "as I hardly ever find time to get down to Brighton. But I can see now that has been only to my great misfortune."

Caroline blushed and giggled prettily, and Annabelle felt something alien and unpleasant stirring in her breast. Caroline, with her blonde curls and sapphire-blue tulle gown, presented an alluring picture amidst all the finery. And Annabelle could not help but notice Devon had made no effort to come up with one of his usual clumsy remarks when greeting her.

The young Arnold, blushing to the roots of his fawn-colored hair, stammered, "W-would you d-do me the honor of this d-dance, Miss Arnsworth?"

It would have been ungracious of her to refuse, so, masking her reluctance with a dazzling smile, she allowed him to lead her onto the floor. A few moments later she noticed Devon, with Caroline's arm tucked protectively through his, leading her into formation.

Devon was a graceful and adept dancer despite reports to the contrary, and despite all attempts not to, Annabelle could not help noticing he appeared to have the coquettish Miss Beckett utterly charmed. Her tinkling laughter reached Annabelle across the floor, and when she turned her head to follow the sound it was she who almost tripped over her own train. And, as fate would have it, it was Devon who next partnered her in the brief rotating turn of the dance. "Mind your steps, Miss Arnsworth," he said, his eyes twinkling. "This floor is uncommonly slippery."

Their gloved fingers touched briefly in the counterturn, and she replied stiffly, "I am pleased to see you do not seem to be suffering too extremely while 'exerting yourself' to please your aunt."

"I make it a policy," he returned lightly as they separated, "never to cause myself unnecessary misery in the course of performing an obligation."

No sooner had young Arnold returned her to her seat than another young gentleman appeared and begged to be presented to her. She had been warned by Lady Marbrough never to dance more than once with the same gentleman, and so she danced five more sets with different partners before supper and felt herself to be quite the belle of the ball. In fact, had her attention not been occupied so much with constantly ascertaining the activities of two persons—Devon and the horrible Mr. Dosset—she would have found herself enjoying a thoroughly pleasant time.

The whereabouts of the first party were never too difficult to ascertain—when he was not making a complete fool of himself with Caroline, he was huddling over the punch bowl with a cluster of other young men, laughing and talking boisterously. He seemed to have an unquenchable thirst, and although she had tasted very little, Annabelle was beginning to suspect the punch contained ingredients far more substantial than wine and fruit. Lady Marbrough's occasional worried glances in that direction confirmed her suspicions, and Annabelle thought that as he would be obligated to take his aunt into supper, the stern lecture Lady Marbrough was no doubt waiting until that moment to deliver would be by then long overdue.

On the matter of Bertram Dosset, she was just allowing herself to relax in the confidence that he might not have come at all, for she had heretofore seen no sign of him. But she was not to be so fortunate, for just as the company was rising to go in for supper, he suddenly appeared at her side. He bowed first to Lady Marbrough, who appeared a little flustered at his presence, and then to Annabelle.

"My dear Miss Arnsworth," he said. "It is quite impossible that you have grown even more lovlier in the hours since we parted. Although," he added with that familiar insinuating gleam, "why I should be surprised I cannot say. You seem to change every time we meet."

Annabelle rose to the occasion with a cool smile. "How very gallant you are, Mr. Dosset." She had come to the conclusion that if he could be bluffed, she would try to do it. And perhaps if she could continue to bluff long enough, he would eventually back down. He certainly could not be confident in his assumption about her identity, or else why would he have waited so long to expose her? In short, as long as she could keep a cool front and make no slips to betray herself, she had the advantage, and she was quite willing to play his game for as long as it took.

"Alas," he continued, "I am late—a most unfortunate habit of mine for which I have already made profuse apologies to my hostess . . . But not too late, I hope," he suggested, extending his arm to Annabelle, "to take you in for supper?"

Annabelle cast her eyes about the room for Devon, and when she found him with Caroline on his arm, leading her toward the supper room, she placed her own hand atop Bertram's arm and responded, "I would be delighted, Mr. Dosset."

He piled her plate high with tiny shrimp and succulent crab in a thick sauce, asparagus tips and jellies and three kinds of cakes, and Annabelle found it very easy to imitate Lucretia's coquettish giggle. "I do believe you are trying to make me fat, Mr. Dosset!"

"That is one transformation," he assured her with a smile, "which I doubt even *you* could accomplish." And he guided her toward a small arbor decked with potted flowers, where a divan had been set up near a small table just large enough for two.

Annabelle was vaguely alarmed, for she had not counted upon being in seclusion with him. "Are you certain this is quite proper?" she suggested. "Ought we not go out and sit with the others?"

"Nonsense," he declared, taking her plate from her and depositing it on the table. "I have, through my own foolishness, already deprived myself of several hours of your company and I am much too selfish to share you now."

Rather than make a scene, she sat down upon the edge of the tufted sofa, and he spread her napkin over her knees. "And now," he said, sitting beside her so closely that she had to edge away, "I have a very special favor to ask. In fact, two favors."

Annabelle speared her shrimp and invited, "Oh?" hoping her nervousness did not show.

"The first is, I understand there will be a waltz after supper. Will you save it for me?"

Annabelle's relief was overwhelming, and she laughed a little. "A simple little dance? What great store you set by my favors!"

His returned smile was cool and rather mirthless. "Yes. A simple dance. Will you?"

She smiled, feeling quite heady with a sense of victory. He was harmless, after all. "I believe that could be managed."

"You are too kind. And the second is," he continued intrepidly, "would you perhaps allow me to call on you while you are here in Brighton?"

Annabelle swallowed hard and took a sip of her wine. Above all else, it was to her advantage to see as little of Bertram Dosset as possible, and the best thing to do was to make every effort to nip their unfortunate relationship in the bud. But she was not entirely certain that was a wise thing to do. She said, recalling instruction given to Lucretia long ago, "Mr. Dosset, you have quite taken me by surprise. Do you not think it a bit bold to presume upon our so brief acquaintance—"

"Of course I would seek permission from your guardian first," he assured her, and she did not know what else to say.

She was rescued at that moment by a most unexpected event. A voice so loud and a tone so slurred as to be hardly recognizable came from over her shoulder, and when she turned it was Devon who was exclaiming, "Here they are!" with a giggling Caroline close at his heels.

He was already well on his way toward what promised to be a most unhappy state. His hair was tousled, his cravat coming undone from its impeccable knot, the top button of his waistcoat was unfastened. He held an overfilled plate in one hand and a glass of wine in the other, and the balance of neither seemed to be too secure. Caroline, perhaps just a little tipsy herself, seemed to notice nothing amiss, and Annabelle glared at them both, more outraged than grateful for the interruption.

"I say, Dosset, we have looked all over for you," Devon exclaimed loudly. "Where've you been hiding? Is there room for us there at your table?"

Bertram half rose and managed a stiff smile. "Lanson," he acknowledged briefly.

Devon looked at Annabelle and then at Bertram and said sincerely, "I do say, we're not interrupting anything here, are we? No *tête-à-tête?* You don't mind if we join you?" As he spoke he leaned a little toward Bertram as though to engage his confidence, his glass tipped, but Bertram moved too quickly for him. However, a few drops of the wine splattered on his coat.

"Oh, I do say, old chap," exclaimed Devon, hastily setting aside the plate and glass as Bertram began to dab at the stain with a napkin, "what a shame! It's not spoilt or anything, is it? It would be a pity if you had to leave when you've only just arrived!"

Bertram managed in a strained tone, "No, no, it's quite all right—"

And Caroline chimed in, "No, Bertie, not that way. Cold water on wine, Mama always says—"

And Annabelle found herself sandwiched in between them, with Devon on one side and Caroline on the other, all ministering to the same ineffectual stain, and heads were beginning to turn. "I assure you," said Bertram, trying to rise, "it is nothing. But as you can see, there is not room for us all at this table—"

Just then a servant appeared with a glass of water and a fresh napkin, and Bertram managed to extricate himself for more professional attentions. Devon said, "You won't hold a grudge will you, old chap? I say, just to make sure of it, you must join us on a little expedition I have planned for a fortnight hence. I've already talked of it to Miss Arnsworth and Caro here, and they both think it's a capital idea."

"I'll check my calendar," replied Bertram distractedly, brushing away the servant and inspecting the damage to his coat. "I'm sure something can be arranged."

"Fine, then," declared Devon, "and we have a party! Now, come, finish your supper while we discuss the details."

Bertram looked at him for a moment and returned with all the politeness he could muster, "You and Miss Beckett are welcome to this table. I believe Miss Arnsworth would enjoy dining elsewhere." He extended his hand to her, and Annabelle hesitated.

"Now, don't go off in a huff," drawled Devon and without pretense or shame drew a thin flask from his waistcoat and poured its contents liberally into his wine. "Come have a spot of a little something which will put your spirits to rights."

Bertram smiled mirthlessly and helped Annabelle to ease past Caroline out of her seat. "Thank you, no. And might I suggest, Mr. Lanson, for your own well-being, you mind your cups?"

Devon leaned back in his seat sloppily. "I'll have you know, sir," he asserted belligerently, "that I can hold my drink as well as any man in this room!"

Bertram nodded and responded pleasantly, "I am quite certain of it. You will excuse us . . ."

Annabelle fanned herself furiously as he led her away, and it was a moment before she could suggest, "Perhaps you had best take me to Lady Marbrough."

"Of course," he agreed sympathetically. "How distressing for you to have to witness such a display. But," he added with an endearing smile, "you will not forget your promise?"

"Promise?" she repeated, baffled.

"The waltz."

"Oh, yes," she answered absently, searching for Lady Marbrough. "Yes, of course." What she was really thinking was that, intoxicated or no, he had called Caroline "Caro." And on such brief acquaintance!

But then she became preoccupied with hopes that Lady Marbrough had not discovered how close her nephew was coming to disgracing her again. Not long after supper those hopes were shattered.

As the hour progressed toward midnight, the dancing became more festive, developing into jigs and reels, and Devon threw himself into them with enthusiasm, tossing his head back and laughing loudly and appearing more than a little unsteady on his feet. More than once Annabelle's sharp eyes caught the appearance of the little brown flask. In short, he was making a spectacle of himself, and the fact could not escape Lady Marbrough's notice.

True to her breeding, Lady Marbrough did not let the agony of embarrassment she must have been experiencing show but only commented once, "I am becoming somewhat concerned for Devon's behavior. I wonder if I should ask Captain Wesley to speak with him?"

"Speak with me about what, madam?" inquired Devon, just then appearing at her elbow and, without waiting for a reply, bowed carelessly to Annabelle. "The most beautiful young lady present here this evening has not danced with me once. Shall we rectify the situation immediately?"

Annabelle drew a breath, contorted her face into a poisonous smile, and replied, "I can think of nothing which would please me more."

As the first chords sounded and they made their bows, he swayed dangerously toward her. Annabelle swept up her train and stepped quickly out of his way. "You will watch where you tread, sir," she muttered through clenched teeth as their fingers touched, "or I swear before all it will be *you* who is embarrassed within an inch of his life this evening!"

He threw back his head and laughed uproariously.

At last the horrid configuration of complicated steps ended and he made to return her to his aunt. But with a deft maneuver which he seemed not to notice, she guided his steps in the other direction. "If you please, sir," she demanded quietly, when they were out of hearing of the other couples, "I will have your flask."

He stared at her innocently, his cravat askew, swaying slightly on his feet.

"It is in your breast pocket," she continued in a careful undertone. "Pray give it to me immediately."

Sullenly, he withdrew the flask and held it caressingly between his fingers for a moment. "Come, dear lady," he mumbled, a childish intonation to his voice, "I have but one vice. Is it so dreadful?"

"It is disgusting," she pronounced and presented her hand, palm upward.

After a moment's hesitation he grinned, shrugged,

and placed the flask in her hand. "Do take good care of it," he pleaded before he sauntered off. "It contains the very elixir of life."

Keeping the flask carefully concealed within the folds of her skirt, Annabelle wandered over to a secluded arbor, opened the flask and brought it delicately to her nostrils. She hesitated, a puzzled frown creasing her brow, and then sniffed again. She turned, looking around for Devon, but he was nowhere to be found. Then, biting her inner lip on the threat of a smile, she deliberately emptied the contents of the flask into a potted plant and hid the incriminating flask itself inside her reticule. She returned to Lady Marbrough.

After that Devon was not seen much, and it was of course Bertram who at last brought the news of his whereabouts. "I am afraid, dear ladies," he informed them, "that your escort is several sheets in the wind—if you will pardon the vulgarity, Lady Marbrough. I just passed him dozing in the corridor."

Admirably, Lady Marbrough concealed her distress.

"If you would like," he suggested with every pretense of good will, "I will see that he is returned safely to his lodgings, and will be happy to escort you both home when you are ready to depart."

"Thank you," said Lady Marbrough stiffly, gathering up her skirts, "but we have our own carriage. Perhaps Captain Wesley would be kind enough to help . . ."

The quartet was striking up the notes of a waltz, several couples left the floor, and a few others, mostly the married ones, took up their places. "But surely you are not leaving this moment," protested Bertram to Annabelle. "You promised me this dance!"

Lady Marbrough looked unaccountably shocked. "But, my dear Lucretia—"

Annabelle cast her an apologetic glance as Bertram swept her away, "I did promise!"

The steps were familiar to her, for she and Lucretia had practiced them many times in the empty upstairs nursery. But she had not imagined how it would feel to be held in a man's arms, her body swaying rhythmically with his, and she found the sensation, especially because it was Bertram who held her, distinctly uncomfortable.

She looked around her anxiously, stiffening against the insistence of his arms. "Mr. Dosset," she managed a little breathlessly, "I believe you are holding me too tightly. People are beginning to stare."

He laughed softly and whirled her around with such force that her skirts flew up above her ankles. "That is not why they are staring, little innocent," he said, his eyes dancing wickedly.

Her heart leaped alarmingly in her chest, for just then she had caught a glimpse of Lady Marbrough's horrified face as they sped by on a turn. "Then why?" she demanded, her eyes straining to follow the turn of heads as they passed, the fans which flew up to hide disapproving conferences, the one or two less bold couples who wandered from the floor.

"It is because you dance so divinely," he replied and caught her even closer to him.

She struggled to free herself, almost missing a step.

"Really, Mr. Dosset, I must insist you not hold me so tightly or I will ask to be taken back to Lady Marbrough."

But he only laughed and drew her closer.

And then suddenly, Bertram came to an abrupt stop. Devon was at her side, standing straight and tall, his eyes dark and his face set in formidable lines. His grip on her elbow was firm. "Miss Arnsworth," he said distinctly, "my aunt is ready to leave."

Now other couples were leaving the floor to stare curiously at the trio, and Annabelle looked around her in growing alarm. Bertram protested, "We have not finished our dance!"

Devon turned to him, drawing himself up stiffly, and not a trace of his former disorientation remained. "You have now," he informed Bertram coldly. "And you, sir, may count yourself fortunate that I have considered your reputation as the worst shot in all of England and decided not to call you out." He turned on his heel, giving Annabelle's arm a gentle jerk, but then added over his shoulder with deadly malice, "This time."

Devon urged her away so quickly that she had difficulty keeping up with his long strides, and he said, in that same deadly cold tone he had used with Bertram, "I have already said your good-byes to our hostess and sent for the carriage. My aunt will be waiting."

Although she was baffled by his anger and aware by the passing glances they received that something was dreadfully wrong, she managed to reply mildly, "Well, I daresay I have never seen anyone recover from intoxication quite so quickly."

He stopped in the empty foyer to stare at her with a mixture of wrath and disappointment, and he returned sharply, "Your conduct tonight was enough to sober a sailor. You dare to speak to me in such a high-and-mighty tone regarding the distress *I* might cause my aunt—have you any idea what your inexcusable behavior has done to her?"

"Inexcusable—?" she gasped, in a temper now herself. "Although I am quite sure I haven't the faintest notion what you are talking about, nothing in my behavior tonight could have equaled yours!"

"Some things," he replied shortly, ushering her into the night air, "are accepted from a gentleman which are unforgivable in a young lady."

In the stiff silence which filled Lady Marbrough's carriage, she demanded, "At least tell me of what I am accused before sending me to the gallows. What have I done which was so shocking?"

In the light of the carriage lamps, Devon's eyes gleamed coldly. It was he who answered, "No young lady dances the waltz without permission from a select group of chaperones—never on her first evening out—and most certainly never with a man like Bertram Dosset."

Annabelle said weakly, "Oh," and sank back against the cushions.

Lady Marbrough blurted shakily, "No, no, Devon, we musn't be harsh with her. It was my fault. Clearly she did not know—she couldn't have known . . . Surely everyone will understand that."

Annabelle offered sincerely, "I am sorry, Lady Marbrough. I truly did not know."

After a moment, Lady Marbrough reached over and patted her hand reassuringly. "Of course you did not, my dear. I am certain we can bring everything to rights."

But the remainder of the journey home was distinctly uncomfortable.

Devon came inside and suggested, as a servant relieved them of their light evening wraps, "Perhaps a glass of Madeira, auntie, to soothe the nerves?"

"My nerves, for one, could use some soothing," she replied with a meaningful glance at him, "but not in that fashion. I believe I will simply retire to my chambers."

"Then you do not mind if I serve myself." He kissed her lightly on the cheek.

"By all means, do as you please," Lady Marbrough replied with a weary sigh. "You will, despite all my advice to the contrary."

For a moment Annabelle stood uncertainly in the hall, positive that only Lady Marbrough's shattered state of mind could have persuaded her to leave them unchaperoned. But when, without ceremony, Devon went into the parlor to pour himself a glass of wine, she followed.

She crossed to the center of the room, not knowing why she lingered and undecided whether to sit or to stand. Devon turned, noticed her, and offered, "May I pour you a glass, Miss Arnsworth?" She refused and he added, "I am certain that you do not come from a family which encourages loose conduct, but you surely realize you should not be down here alone with me."

She smiled a little wanly. "Somehow I feel quite safe in the assurance that you will not take advantage of me."

The way his hand tighted abruptly about the glass as he lifted it to his lips caused a sudden and not altogether unpleasant lurching in her heart. "And if I were otherwise inclined?" he said, and drank deeply.

She forced herself to wander over to the prim chair she had occupied that afternoon and sat down casually. "As I said," she replied, "I do not think so. But then I might be mistaken, for you are a most peculiar man. For example"—she glanced at him—"although I have heard of the drastic measures gentlemen sometimes take to escape an unpleasant situation, I have never before known one who chooses to drown his sorrows in lemonade." She held out his flask.

For a moment she caught his startled expression, and then his features smoothed into the beginnings of a smile. He took the flask from her and tucked it into his pocket. "So," he said softly, "you knew all along."

"Not all along," she admitted honestly.

He looked at her, his gaze intent and searching, and she felt her feelings rising to a breathless pitch, as though in response to a caress. And he said quietly, "Nothing I do dismays you, does it?"

She answered evenly, her own longing shining uncontrollably in her eyes, "No."

The glass was deposited on the mantel, swiftly he

crossed the room, and his face as he bent over her was so intense that for a moment it frightened her. "For God's sake, Lucretia," he said softly, his eyes rapidly and insistently scanning hers, "if you wanted to waltz, why did you not ask me?"

His hands were warm upon her shoulders, gently drawing her to her feet, slipping about her waist and clasping her one hand in the position of the dance. And as he drew her close, the silk of her bodice pressing against his strong broad chest, she yielded breathlessly to the starburst of sensations his presence created. His intense, searching eyes never left hers, his firmly molded mouth was only inches above hers, and by fractions, he closed the distance. Then, just before she felt the brush of his lips upon hers, before that delicious moment of cascading yearning was satisfied, as her heart was pounding in her ears and the frightful but wonderful excitement was rushing through her veins, he suddenly stiffened and she thought she heard the one word, "No."

He stepped away, his face had gone hard and his eyes remote. "I bid you good evening, Miss Arnsworth," he said coolly and turned to go.

So shocked was she that she could not utter a word of protest or question, but simply watched in stunned disbelief as he crossed the room and closed the door on his exit. In another moment, when she heard the outer door close behind him, she could only sink weakly to the chair, a keener despair than any she had ever known seeping through her.

She had been wrong to admit so quickly there was nothing he could do to dismay her.

CHAPTER 6

The next afternoon, while the town was lazily recovering from the festivities of the night before, Annabelle went with Caroline to the circulating library in search of a book. It was not by any means that Caroline was inclined to read or professed the slightest enthusiasm for the literary pursuits, but her mother, she explained, had expressed the desire for a light novel or two to pass the time while she was confined indoors with a cold and it provided Caroline with the opportunity for some exercise—and also her favorite pastime, gossip.

She was dressed smartly in a chic walking outfit of her favorite sapphire blue, accented with an emerald-green cape and streamers and an enchanting little bonnet of a darker green lined with rows of sapphire ruching. Caroline was well aware that the color suited her golden curls and accented her large blue eyes perfectly, and she took fine advantage of the fact, strolling at a leisurely pace which allowed her to bow deeply and return the greetings of every complimentary young man who passed.

Annabelle could not imagine why the brilliant Caro had sought her particular company, unless it was the fact that on this day, after a restless night in which sleep had come only with the pink light of an eastern sky, Annabelle's plainness and almost careless toilette could only set off Caroline's beauty by comparison. She dressed modestly, for she had learned that the circulating library was a fashionable gathering place for bored aristocrats during the hot summer days, and it was wise, after the fiasco of the previous evening, not to draw too much attention to herself right away.

"That nasty Bertie," confessed Caroline as she returned a polite nod to a passing matron, "knew very well that you had not been brought out in London and that it would be taboo for you to waltz . . ." She hiked up her skirts with a glare as an inconsiderate horseman passed too close to their path. "Furthermore, he knew that you did *not* know, so do not allow him to tell you otherwise. I have known him since we were children, and this is just the sort of prank he would pull." She linked her arm through Annabelle's with a not-too-sincere squeeze of sympathy. "Poor Lucretia! Wouldn't it be just too terrible for words if you were ruined your very first night out?"

Annabelle managed a stiff smile. "I hardly think it can be quite that serious."

"Oh, but it is!" Caroline assured her. "Why, the matrons are stricter here than in London, if you can believe it, and I've no doubt that before the day is done at least three of them will have written to your mother . . ."

Annabelle stopped abruptly with the impact of this new and horrible possibility. But Caroline soothed, "Or perhaps not, out of respect to Lady Marbrough . . . I shouldn't let it distress me if I were you."

"No, it's not that," Annabelle answered a little weakly.

"I've just only remembered I need to post a letter. Could we cross over here?"

Yes, indeed, it would be too terrible for words should her aunt call her home now, although yesterday she might have conceded that it was all for the best. More than anything else, it was necessary that she stay, for if she left now she would never see Devon again . . .

It was quite impossible, but undeniably true—she had fallen head over heels in love with the very man she had come here prepared to despise. Her pact with Lucretia had been to discourage him, but she found herself now longing for only a glimpse of him, her heart racing in that foolish counterrhythm whenever she thought of him, knowing that she would be content to spend the rest of her days gazing at him if only from a distance . . . precisely like one of those heroines in a silly romantic novel.

And, oh, what a wretched tangle of possibilities this produced! For, though it must break her heart, she must keep her promise to Lucretia and do everything within her power to make certain that, by summer's end, Devon Lanson was totally indifferent to whether or not he ever encountered Lucretia Arnsworth again. And the worst of it was, paradoxically, that the task would be an easy one. For he had proven last evening, in the moment that had forever changed Annabelle's life, how simple he would find it to forget her.

On their way again, Caroline turned to the subject which Annabelle least wanted to discuss. "Mr. Lanson can really be most charming, can he not? I can't think how he obtained such a foul reputation. Although"—she giggled a little—"perhaps he did overdo himself a bit last evening and my mother was not at *all* pleased, let me tell you that, but I had only to remind her of what a perfect fool Papa can make of himself on court day and of the way Arnold disgraced himself all over the carpet at my coming-out party and she closed her lips on *that* subject pretty quickly! She agreed," she announced primly, "that he may call on me."

Annabelle for some reason found it difficult to reply, "And do you think he will?"

"But of course," she answered airily. "He danced with me twice, you know, which is all that was proper, *and* took me into supper. It would be the greatest insult if he did not attempt to call." She sighed dreamily. "Isn't it the most fabulous thing," she said, "to be in a position where one is not forced to consider only marriages of convenience?"

Annabelle started at the word "marriage," but Caroline continued obliviously, "Of course, it is a great pity that he is so abominably destitute, but it is not as though my dowry would not more than compensate, and the family name is positively impeccable. I believe there is a title or two floating around there somewhere, though I am not quite clear as to how . . ."

Annabelle interrupted, "I believe we are about to walk past the library," and Caroline giggled.

"Silly me! Well, come along then, I shan't be a moment."

Annabelle followed her up the steps, wondering desolately what Devon would think of the scheming Miss Beckett's plans for his future. Perhaps he would not be so repelled as she might think, for it was an undeniable fact that he must marry for money, and he did appear at least to have found Caroline appealing. The very worst of it was that Annabelle Morgan had no weapons with which to fight back. She was, except for the meager royalties earned by her novel, as poor as a church mouse, and a promise and a secret prevented her.

Caroline soon lost herself in a group of chattery girl-friends anxious to relive in every detail last evening's triumphs, and after a time Annabelle wandered unobtrusively about the shop. At least one good thing would come of this desperate farce—after only three days she was well on her way toward completing her novel, which promised to be even more smashing than the last. With luck, before too many more weeks passed Mr. Addison Fitzroy of Fitzroy, Patterson & Potts, Publishers, would have the second manuscript for which he had been begging her.

Wandering down the aisle of neatly stacked books, she found it at last. It was always a thrill for her to touch it, to hold it in her hand and run her finger down the lines of laboriously penned words now bound into neat print. . . *Patches and Pins,* by A. P. Morgan.

"Lucretia! Oh, Lucretia—look who I've found!"

Annabelle lifted her head to see Caroline gaily approaching and clinging to the arm of Devon Lanson. Again, her heart did that slow, painful turn and then pattered with excitement, and unconsciously she pressed the book over her breast, as though the inexcusable antics within her chest might be seen by the casual observer without its protection.

In his casual afternoon attire, a fawn frock coat and berry-brown riding breeches, his rich brown hair in its perpetual tousled state and the half-light of a lazy smile in his eyes, he was even more devastating than he had been the evening before. Annabelle clutched the book more tightly to her chest.

"Miss Arnsworth." He bowed to her. "You look charming this afternoon." And as he raised his head she imagined a faint mocking gleam there, for she knew she looked nothing of the sort.

She replied acidly, "And how well you have recovered from last evening's indulgence, Mr. Lanson."

He ignored the remark and fastened instead upon the book. "What is that you're reading?"

He reached for it and she passed it into his hands. "Do you read, Mr. Lanson?"

"Quite a lot, actually," he replied, and as he opened the cover the expression which darkened his face was unmistakably a scowl.

Caroline, unaware, said gaily, "I find reading such an exclusively *gentlemanly* pursuit. My papa is forever cloistered in that frightfully oppressive library of his, but as for myself I can scarce be around more than two books at a time without feeling positively giddy! Perhaps you and he might enjoy a bookish discussion some time, Mr. Lanson."

"Indeed we might," he answered absently and then closed the book with a snap and abruptly returned it to its shelf. "However, I am quite certain that one of the readings we will not be discussing is *this*."

Immediately all of Annabelle's defensive instincts

bristled. She retrieved the volume. "Oh?" she demanded. "And why is that?"

"I must say, Miss Arnsworth," he returned evenly, "you never cease to shock me. I would have thought your mother's good breeding and my aunt's chaperonage would have discouraged you from the pursuit of filling your mind with such unmitigated trash."

She gasped, "Unmitigated tr—"

"Yes, indeed," he asserted mildly. "I fail to see how anyone of taste could find the caricaturing of some of the country's noblest names in what amounts to little more than a blatant libel entertaining. And as for the type of twisted mind which could actually commit such things to paper . . . in my opinion, Mr. A. P. Morgan should be drawn and quartered."

She stared at him, speechless, and Caroline, with curiosity aroused, took the little volume from her limp fingers. "Oh, I have heard of it!" She giggled delightedly. "It is supposed to be *quite* scandalous, you know. Why," she lowered her voice to a conspiratorial whisper, "I have heard that A. P. Morgan is actually a pseudonym and that the author is in fact one of our very own set, lurking about and gathering up juicy bits of gossip . . . isn't that just too dastardly for words?"

"My sentiments exactly," agreed Devon heartily. "The sort of freakish devil who would stoop so low for a bit of profit epitomizes to me the worst sort of traitor."

Annabelle managed, "I understand his book has a very wide circulation."

"Which is a sad comment on our society."

"I believe the book in itself," responded Annabelle,

disguising the fraying of her own temper rather poorly, "is intended to be a comment on our 'sad society.'"

"Don't be absurd! Haven't we enough problems, internal and external, without having them flaunted in our face by some ne'er-do-well?"

"My, my," murmured Annabelle, lowering her eyes briefly to hide the dangerous spark there, "I had no idea you spoke so eloquently on the subject of domestic affairs. What a pity you haven't a seat in the House of Lords"—now she slanted those snapping eyes toward him—"or perhaps the House of Commons."

His jaw tightened and his eyes darkened as his hands clenched to forceful fists at his sides. "Merely because I do not sit, Miss Arnsworth, is no reason to assume I can forget my rightful heritage—no more than should you. Our families are what make this nation great, and every time we cast our eyes upon such"—he gave the book which Caroline held loosely a distasteful flick with his fingers before pronouncing distinctly—"garbage, we are undermining that greatness and casting aspersions on our own heritage." He fixed her with a withering stare. "It is a matter of pride which you, Miss Arnsworth, may take lightly, but which I can assure you I most certainly do not."

"Oh, dear . . ." Caroline looked quite out of place and very much at a loss, caught between their crossfire. She hastily returned the volume to the stack on the table and suggested, "Might we not do better by moving on to lighter subjects?"

After a moment Annabelle saw his taut, broad shoulders relax suddenly, the dark disapproval fade from his face to be replaced by a more equable expression, and he replied politely, "Once again I have broken a cardinal rule of polite behavior—a gentleman must never discuss intellectual pursuits with a lady." He smiled enchantingly at Caroline. "I have bored Miss Beckett and most likely made an enemy of Miss Arnsworth for life. Will you forgive me?"

Caroline giggled and demurred, and Annabelle replied stuffily, "It is a silly rule, designed, I think, to suit those gentlemen who fear they will always come off the worse in any such discussion."

He acknowledged her comment with a slight lift of the eyebrow and nothing more. "Nonetheless, I do apologize. Will you allow me to make amends by escorting you lovely ladies home?"

Caroline was quick to latch on to his arm, Annabelle accepted somewhat more reluctantly. Even with the sparks of her temper only just beginning to die down, the feel of his powerful muscle beneath her light touch had its thrilling and despairing effect on her, and she was lost in her own blue fog as he kept up a cheerful chatter of inanities with Caroline on the way home. How could she love a man who was so arrogant, hotheaded, and mean? How could she possibly have allowed herself to fall so desperately for a man who, it turned out, held her very life's work in despite?

But the fact was that she did, and she was very much afraid nothing he or she could say or do would ever change the fact.

He left her at Lady Marbrough's door, for Caroline's house was the last to be reached, with no more than a casual reminder of the excursion scheduled for two weeks from the day. Annabelle went inside and removed her cape and gloves with uncontrollably bitter reflections as to how much ground the enterprising Caroline could cover in the brief walk from this house to hers.

Her hostess was in the parlor, writing at the desk, and the first thing which caught Annabelle's attention was an enormous vase of deep pink sweetheart roses, replicas of the ones Devon had given her the night before and the bud she had worn in her gown. She went over to them with an exclamation of delight, inhaling the scent as she caressed the petals.

Lady Marbrough turned with a smile and said, "Yes, my dear, you have had a caller. But first sit down and let me tell you all the news. I am so glad you have returned —did you have a pleasant excursion?"

"Very nice, thank you," replied Annabelle, searching the flowers for a card. But they had to be from Devon. And he had not said a word of it! Her fingers tingled with excitement and she felt a pretty blush rising to her cheeks to match the shade of the roses. Of course they were from Devon!

"Do sit down, my dear," urged Lady Marbrough. "That can wait."

Reluctantly, Annabelle did as she was bid, but found it hard to keep her eyes off the bouquet and the promise it held.

"The most marvelous thing," announced Lady Marbrough. "I have had Mrs. Wesley and Lady Rounston and Lady Balfort over to tea and they have decided that, under the circumstances, it would be quite improper to censure your behavior of last evening."

"Oh." Annabelle tried hard to sound gracious. "How very kind of them, I am sure."

"I merely explained," continued Lady Marbrough with the air of one relating a great triumph, "how very difficult it is to bring out marriageable young ladies these days, with great emphasis upon your complete innocence in the entire matter, and they agreed that it would be a great shame to ruin your chances over such a small indiscretion. And of course, when one takes into consideration your unusual background and the fact that the impropriety did not occur in London where, I'm afraid, it simply could not be forgiven, allowances must be made."

"I am very pleased, Lady Marbrough," Annabelle answered sincerely. "I would not wish to think anything I have done would repay your hospitality with shame."

Lady Marbrough smiled, obviously pleased with herself and her charge. "I am only now writing to your mother to explain the situation, for she is bound to hear of it sooner or later. I have every reason to believe all will come to rights."

"That is wonderful. Thank you."

And then Lady Marbrough hesitated and frowned slightly. "The young gentleman involved—Mr. Dosset—did apologize quite eloquently, claiming that he had no knowledge of his wrong . . . That, of course, I do not believe for a moment, but I must say he appeared to be genuinely repentant."

Annabelle grew alert. "Mr. Dosset was here?"

"Yes, my dear," answered Lady Marbrough impatiently. "That is what I am telling you. He asked permission to call on you, but I had to think that would not be quite proper. I saw no reason, however, to keep you from the outing you have arranged with Devon already, at which he will be present, nor to prevent you from dancing with him again should he ask—only in the accepted fashion, of course."

Annabelle said weakly, "I see."

"He asked to leave this note for you," said Lady Marbrough, producing it from her desk, "and I could find no objection. In fact, after all that Devon has said about him, I must say I was both surprised and impressed with his manner of address. But blood will tell, I suppose, and he is from a very fine family."

Hesitantly, Annabelle took the card, and as she read her heart seemed to sink to the very tips of her embroidered kid slippers. "My dearest Miss Arnsworth," it read. "I have been unable to remove the scent or the sight of these delicate blossoms from my mind since they enchanted me in your presence last evening. It is my fervent hope that they will bring you as much pleasure as the memory of them has brought me, and that you will accept this humble offering with my most profuse apologies for any unintentional distress I might have caused you. I remain your most devoted servant, Bertram Amory Dosset."

Annabelle folded the card quietly and her eyes fell on the vase of roses which no longer seemed quite so alluring. In her room upstairs, pressed between the covers of a treasured volume of poetry, was the nosegay Devon had given her last night. And she knew that, in a choice between the elaborate bouquet now before her and the small knot of wilting blossoms which was preserved upstairs, she far preferred the offering of the simpler man.

CHAPTER 7

A letter came from Lucretia:

"Dearest Annabelle—I was so pleased to hear how well everything is going, as I never had a doubt it would. And pray, do not fret, as I am taking the *utmost* care in posting my letter, and have been very clever about reading Mama's out loud to her. She has already received several with a Brighton direction regarding some nonsense about a supposed indiscretion with a waltz, but I covered that quite well, I thought. Honestly, my dearest Bella, you will drive yourself to old age with worry! Has not everything so far gone as smoothly as I promised?

"Almost I envy you the parties and the gaiety but that I know you deserve the fun much more than I and besides I would not trade one moment in my beloved Freddy's company for a year of balls and galas! He took me riding yesterday . . ."

Annabelle, reading the letter for the second time, skipped over that part.

"As to the matter of Mr. Bertram Dosset, it is most peculiar that you should ask, as by chance I had my first and only encounter with said person less than a month ago and found him to be a *most* disagreeable man. He was quite forward, in fact, and asked permission to call on me. Mama, of course, refused forthrightly. She called him, quite correctly I believe, a fortune hunter, and hinted at some scandal which has been so well hushed up not even she knows all the details. At any rate, it is a great pity, for he comes from quite a respectable family which he has all but brought to ruin with his gaming and loose living and, I understand, has brought his poor papa nothing but debts and his mother only shame and his sister may not even be brought out next season because of it. And his cousin, Lowrey Knox—you recall Lowrey, do you not?—he has finally come to the point with Chloe, can you imagine, and their engagement is expected to be announced at the ball this month (perhaps, with any fortune at all, there will be more than *one* such announcement on that occasion!!)—at any rate, Lowrey is such a perfectly *presentable* young man and so retiring, one would never guess what black sheep lurked in the back of his family closet, would one? Mama says it happens in the best of families, but I cannot but find such matters ultimately distasteful, don't you agree?

"Speaking of distasteful matters, I do extend my sympathies to you regarding Mr. Lanson, for he sounds to be a most horrid man! However, dearest, you are so clever I have no doubt but that you will have discovered a way to knock him for a turn before the week is out, and at least you do not have to concern yourself with a marriage proposal from the wretched creature!

"Dearest, dearest Annabelle, my mind is in a whirl, for I have just seen Freddy ride up and my heart practically leaps to my throat even as I write . . . Darling, go out and have simply *loads* of fun, and I will love you forever for what you are doing for me this summer . . . I will name my first daughter for you! (With Freddy's permission, of course.) I always did say you were the strongest, cleverest, bravest girl who ever lived and there is simply no one else in whom I can place my trust! With loads of hugs and kisses, I remain forever your adoring Lucy."

It was nine o'clock in the morning and Annabelle was already dressed in the smart forest-green riding habit Lucretia had insisted she pack, waiting for Devon's arrival at a time when most of the town was just beginning to make its first sleepy stirrings into a new day. She thoughtfully folded the letter and hid it once again well to the back of her writing case, already forming a reply in the back of her head. So much had changed since the posting of Annabelle's original letter a fortnight ago! Dared she tell Lucy of the changed circumstances regarding Devon Lanson? No, it would only confuse her unnecessarily, and it would do Annabelle no service to put on paper the hopelessness of an unattainable love. And one might have thought that Lucy, silly as she was, would have gathered from Annabelle's inquiry about Bertram Dosset that she had actually met the person, with all the danger that entailed. But no—Lucy, her head filled with orange blossoms, had allowed that detail to completely slip past her and maintained her cheerful optimism to the end.

No, the problem of Bertram Dosset was one with which she would have to deal herself, and with each new scrap of information she gleaned about him, the project became both more challenging and frightening. It puzzled her that her aunt, who was the most gullible soul alive, had been sufficiently struck by his conduct or his reputation to refuse to allow him to call upon her daughter. To Annabelle's knowledge that was the first time ever that so drastic a step had been taken, for, despite outside opinions, Lucretia's mother *was* concerned with her daughter's marriageability and never lost an opportunity to make her known to any eligible gentleman of quality and name. But she apparently did not consider the situation desperate enough to encourage such as Bertram Dosset, family and title notwithstanding.

That he was known for passionate gaming and indiscretion did not surprise her, such was the vice of the young gentlemen of many noble families, and although such conduct was not approved, it certainly was not enough to permanently soil a reputation. Again and again she had caught references to the "scandal" which was so unmentionable no one seemed to know the whole of it and which, contrarily, had been so well suppressed it had not yet ostracized Bertram from society. With some trepidation, Annabelle was aware of a burning need to know more about that particular portion of her nemesis' background.

She heard horse's hooves on the pavement below and the sound of light laughter, and, peeking out the window, she saw her party had arrived, with Devon just alighting from the saddle. Quickly she gathered up her gloves and crop and stole quietly out so as not to disturb the sleeping Lady Marbrough. Then she ran lightly down the stairs and arrived in the front hall just as Braddock opened the door to Devon.

He looked at her for a moment with an approval in his eyes which made her spirits soar and brought a becoming color to her cheeks beneath the dainty green cloche with its yellow feather which rested atop her curls. But in the end all he said was, "Good. You did not keep us waiting," and turned to usher her outside. "I have chosen quite a nice young mare for you," he added as they crossed the walk to where Bertram and Caroline were waiting with the horses. "I hope she will not be too spirited for you to handle."

"I have the utmost confidence in you as a judge of horseflesh," she returned brightly, but eyed with some dismay the glossy chestnut who was tossing her bridle impatiently.

"Good morning, Miss Arnsworth," called Bertram from the saddle and started to dismount. "How very pleasing you look today."

"No, please—keep your mount." She tried to disguise the anxiety in her eyes. "I believe Mr. Lanson is in somewhat of a hurry to be off."

"Indeed yes," replied Devon, grasping her waist to assist her into the sidesaddle with no more intimacy than one might show to a sack of flour while performing the same action. So unlike the last time. "If we wait much longer the tide will begin to return and we will be bogged down."

"Naughty Caro," teased Bertram, "kept us waiting half an hour on her front lawn."

Caroline laughed lightly. "I can't recall when I have

seen this hour of morning before! My, everything looks so different, does it not?"

Devon swung easily astride his own powerful black stallion and took up the reins. "Are we ready?"

Annabelle swallowed hard, grasped her own reins firmly with both hands, and nodded. Devon, at the head of the little caravan, urged his horse into a brisk trot.

Caroline drew up beside her and said, "Isn't this the most splendid adventure? We are going to ride along the beach all the way to the old lighthouse in New-haven and have a picnic nuncheon there."

Annabelle, whose grasp of regional geography was not perfect, nonetheless knew that Newhaven must be ten miles from their present position, assuming one took a straight course to the beach. She managed, trying to be a sport, "The lighthouse? Isn't that rather far?"

Bertram, coming up beside her, said, "Do not fret, fair lady. You have two strong protectors to guard you every step of the way."

Caroline, with one of her familiar pouts, urged her horse ahead, leaving Annabelle alone with Bertram.

"I was beginning to fear you had not forgiven me," said Bertram mildly over the gentle clip-clop of their horses' hooves in the still morning air. "You have done all but snub me at every affair we have attended this past fortnight."

"While it was not my intention to snub you," she replied coolly, "I am not quite certain I should forgive you, either. That was quite a nasty trick you played on me at the Wesley reception."

"My dear lady," he exclaimed dramatically, "I assure

you it was not my intention to do anything of the sort! I protest my innocence most sincerely!"

Annabelle glanced at him askance and answered, "Then it is two of us who are the victims of an unhappy circumstance."

"Wronged in camaraderie," he agreed with a heavy sigh. "Then why will you not allow me to call on you? Must I needs pay for a simple mistake forever?"

"My chaperone," said Annabelle, her eyes fixed straight ahead on the backs of Devon and Caroline, who seemed to be engaged in quite an amusing conversation, "does not think it proper that we should be seen in company so soon."

He seemed to ponder this for a moment, and when he spoke there was something in his tone which was not quite pleasant, despite its assumed mildness. "Then we will certainly have to do something to change her mind, will we not?"

Annabelle glanced at him, and his eyes were cold and calculating. They were the eyes of a man who was not accustomed to having his will thwarted. Clumsily, she spurred her horse and put quick distance between them.

As they came on to the beach they could no longer ride four abreast because of the lapping surf, and though she was not quite certain how it came about, Caroline paired with Bertram and it was Devon who rode beside her. She understood now why Lady Marbrough had been so set against this adventure. Only an experienced horseman could with any accuracy guide his mount over the pebbles and bits of broken shale, around protruding stones and through the sucking sand.

Though neither Caroline nor Bertram seemed to be having difficulty, Annabelle found herself slowing her mare to a bare walk. Her wrists ached and every muscle in her body was strained with the effort, and she could tell Devon was having to rein in his mount tightly to keep her pace.

"You told me you could ride," he said sternly, in a moment.

She looked at him, tired and impatient and at a distinct disadvantage, for there was no point in issuing a vain disclaimer. "It was no more a fib," she returned shortly, "than a great many things you told me about yourself, which also proved to be untrue."

He reached out a hand to her as her mare threatened to stumble, but she steadied the poor creature without his assistance. "Such as?" he pursued.

She glanced at him miserably. She had gone too far to back down now, and at any rate it hardly mattered. She blurted, "Such as your intense dislike for scheming socialites and your determination not to marry a fortune!"

At first he looked merely startled, and then he stiffened angrily, a dark shield coming over his eyes. "I don't recall ever saying anything of the sort to you."

"Well, it doesn't matter now to whom you said it," she went on heedlessly. "The point is it was said!"

He rode beside her in cold silence for a time, and Annabelle's heart ached. Now what could he think of her but that she was petulant and sharp-tongued, and an eavesdropper as well. When at last he spoke, it was with more equability than she had dared hope for. "Indeed," he said. "And still I do not understand why you should accuse me of having spoken anything which was false."

"I believe that is quite obvious," she answered, "as you have made no effort whatsoever to disguise your attraction to Miss Beckett."

He tossed his head back to the gentle sea breeze and laughed. "A gentleman, Miss Arnsworth," he told her, his eyes sparkling gaily, "even one of so temperate a nature as my own, must have his diversions, must he not?"

"An attraction," she continued in a fierce undertone, although Caroline and Bertram were too far ahead to overhear above the rushing of the surf, "which I feel obliged to point out is returned. I believe Caroline expects you to offer for her before the summer is out."

Abruptly, the mirth disappeared, and his eyes sharpened for a moment before he jerked them away from her face to fasten on the hoofprints in the sand before them. "That," he replied in a subdued tone, "is utter nonsense. Miss Beckett is as fickle and frivolous as any other of the sex."

Was that disappointment she imagined in his voice? Desperately she hoped not. But why else would he have invited Caro, on such short acquaintance, to join him today? And why did his expression grow so strange when she mentioned Caroline's expectations? Why, after exerting such effort, up to and including this abominable excursion, to discourage the designs of Lucretia Arnsworth, did he make no effort to do anything of the sort where Caroline was concerned? There was only one possible answer, and Annabelle felt her spirits sinking as inexorably as were the hooves of her poor mare in the wet sand.

"Perhaps," she said through a rising lump in her throat, "I will just go up and ride with Mr. Dosset and leave you to discuss this matter with Caroline in private."

She made to move her horse forward, but swiftly his hand shot out to close around her wrist, strong and brown against the pale gray of her glove, his grip firm. "You will do nothing of the sort," he told her. "I have advised you before to keep great distance between yourself and Mr. Dosset, and this time I intend to remain close enough to you to see that you do it."

She fell back in some surprise, her former despair all but forgotten. "Then why," she demanded, "did you invite him along in the first place?"

He released her hand, his eyes growing strangely moody as he followed the progress of the couple ahead of them. "Sometimes," he said at last, "it is best to have the enemy under close surveillance."

"Your—enemy, sir?" she queried, growing more and more fascinated.

He glanced at her with a pitying smile. "Not mine, Miss Arnsworth—yours."

She almost lost her breath in the sudden salty breeze which swept a straying curl across her face. She said cautiously, "Mine?"

"You cannot be so innocent," he returned grimly. "Bertram Dosset intends to ruin you if he can, and I do not intend to stand by and watch him take you for prey."

In the set of his mouth was the same expression she recalled with a little thrill from that dreadful night at the Wesley *soirée,* at the moment Devon had threatened to call Bertram out. She had never before so much as dreamt of having a gentleman go to paces in defense of her honor, and though she knew she should find such a spectacle appalling, in fact the thought of it caused her heart to do that peculiar little roll again.

Drawing stern rein on her common sense, she replied, "I assure you Mr. Lanson, I am quite capable of taking care of myself—if I were given only a hint as to what I should be defending myself against. Why do you despise him so?"

For a time he did not answer, and when he did, it was with a gruff "Some things are better left unspoken to untutored ears."

She insisted, "Perhaps my ears are not so untutored as you supposed."

He reined in his horse and turned to her, his eyes angry and his lips taut with repressed emotion. Unconsciously, she shrank back. "Very well, you wish to hear it, then hear it you shall." He spoke in a clipped, precise tone, as though the very words were distasteful to him. "His father's country seat is in North Kent, not far from my home. We are a rather close-knit community there. There was the matter of a local merchant's daughter— quite a respectable family though not particularly well-to-do. He refused to marry her."

Annabelle said in some puzzlement, "That is all? But I don't understand. Why should he be expected to marry . . ." He held her with a steady gaze, and she shut her mouth abruptly, her eyes growing wide.

He turned to gaze over the choppy, blue-green sea. "He disclaimed all responsibility. She drowned herself a month later, and her father never recovered from the shock. She was a decent girl, you see, from a decent family." Now he turned to look at her. "Just like you."

Quickly, she gathered her whirling thoughts and the reins of her horse and they began their steady plod forward. "Thank you for warning me," she managed quietly, in a moment.

"I only hope that now you will take my warning to heart."

But after a time she had to pursue. "I cannot understand how such a—dreadful thing—has failed to come to light."

"His father is a man of some influence," replied Devon soberly, "who has already suffered much from his son. These things can be hushed up for a time, but I doubt that it can be kept quiet much longer unless Bertram makes a profitable match and pursues the appearance of reform." He looked at her, and the gentle depths of his eyes moved her to a quickening response. "That is why I warn you most particularly to take care."

On the breath of a reply, Devon suddenly turned his head in response to a hail from the couple ahead of them. The moment was spoiled, and they quickened their pace to join them.

"Caroline proposes a race," said Bertram, his dark hair whipping across his face with the brisk breeze.

"Only to the promontory just ahead. She maintains she can outrun any of us."

"I will do it, too!" cried Caroline, excitement snapping in her eyes.

"A capital idea!" exclaimed Devon, back in his role. Then he glanced at Annabelle. "Give your mare her head. She will do much better at a brisk run than the staid plod you've been keeping her to."

Bertram called time, and of course he was a length ahead at the outset. Annabelle tensed her body and leaned low, her hands slack on the reins, squinting her eyes against the flying wet sand and the spray of surf as Devon stampeded his stallion into the water, fearing at any moment she would be dashed against the rocks or thrown into the sea. Soon Caroline was ahead, and she tossed a gay laugh over her shoulder, the bright curls dancing in the sunlight, and Annabelle could tell Devon was holding his horse back to let her win.

In just that moment of injured pride she lost her concentration or perhaps communicated her own sense of outrage to her mount, for the poor creature suddenly lurched to the side, caught its forefeet in the sucking tide and went down on its knees. Only good fortune prevented her from being tossed head over heels into the water. As it was, she slid off the mare's side, wrenching her ankle in the stirrup before she could free it, and she could not help crying out.

Immediately the flashing of black hooves and flying sand filled her vision, and Devon was dismounting swiftly and coming toward her, his face pale and his

eyes filled with stark alarm. And he was on his knees
beside her, grasping her arms roughly, his voice husky
with fear as he demanded, "Good God, Lucretia, are
you all right? Are you hurt?"

Except for the vague throbbing in her ankle, Annabelle was feeling only shocked, wet, and foolish. She
managed, "My horse—was she hurt?"

Devon said impatiently, tightening his grip on her
arms, "Never mind about that now—what of you? Are
you hurt?"

"I think—I may have twisted my ankle."

Bertram came forward, leading her mount. "My dear
Miss Arnsworth, what a nasty spill you took! Are you
quite all right?"

"Yes, thank you, I think so . . ."

As cautious relief began to flood Devon's face, he became more brisk and businesslike. "We'd best have a
look at that ankle. Which one is it?"

"No, please," protested Annabelle, feeling more
foolish by the moment. "If I remove my boot it may
begin to swell and I could not get it on again. If you'll
only help me to stand I'm quite sure I will be all
right . . ."

Caroline came running up, and, upon ascertaining
that Annabelle was unhurt, her look of concern faded
into one of patent self-interest, and even though she
offered sympathetically, "What a shame!" her tone indicated she was more sorry for her own spoiled fun than
for Annabelle's misfortune.

"Perhaps you are right about the boot," Devon conceded reluctantly. "We had best wait until we get home and have Dr. Broadstreet look at it."

"I'm sure that won't be necessary," insisted Annabelle. "If only you will help me to my feet . . ."

He slipped his arm about her and guided her gently to her feet, and although Annabelle could not help wincing as her weight rested on her ankle, in the protection of his arms and with his warmth shielding her she felt for the moment secure and delightedly content.

"Perhaps," Devon suggested to Bertram, "you would be good enough to gather some wood for a fire. Miss Arnsworth appears to be quite soaked. I will take her to the shelter of that rock there, out of the breeze."

He helped her to limp up the beach toward the shelter and sat down beside her. "I do feel so foolish," she apologized nervously. "It was all due to my clumsiness, and now there's all this fuss and I have spoiled your expedition."

"There will be the very devil to pay," he agreed, "from my aunt. After she warned me."

But when she looked at him, his lips were curving into a rueful smile, and she returned it with a toasty feeling spreading through her, like a shared intimacy. "I will try," she promised, "to be more adept at heeding warnings than you have been."

For a time they watched Bertram and Caroline walking along the beach, gathering up driftwood, and Devon commented, "Perhaps I should be more concerned over the welfare of Miss Beckett than of yourself."

Annabelle stiffened, the lovely moment gone. "Perhaps you should."

He turned to her directly, his eyes sober and conveying a message which made her throat constrict tightly on the fear of reading too much within them. He said, "I believe you misquoted me a moment ago, on the beach. I did not mean that all aspiring socialites were the same. I merely implied that I find the simpering ways and obsessions of some with absurdities tiresome, and I believe I might once have commented that any young lady who makes a great fuss over a spoilt gown was not worth my trouble."

Annabelle blushed to the tips of her fingers at this, and he commented mildly, "Look at the state your habit is in. I doubt if it can be repaired. What do you think our charming Miss Beckett would do should the same misfortune befall that ridiculous concoction of velvet she is wearing?"

Annabelle thought about this for a moment and was hard put to fight off a fit of the giggles. "Swoon, fly into hysterics, and take to her bed for a week," she decided. "In that order."

He smiled at her and the light from his eyes warmed the depths of her soul. Then she felt his fingers lightly touch hers, the sensation sent a shiver of fire rushing from her fingertips to flood her veins and whirl in her head, and she wanted more than anything to be held in his arms as she had been before, pressed close to him with his face only inches above hers and the passion in his eyes burning promises into her heart. He said softly, "Lucretia, you are quite unlike any woman I have ever known . . ."

She whispered, searching his eyes for more of what she wanted to read there, "Please do not call me that."

And the spell was broken. She felt his hand slip from hers with an awful sense of loss, saw the confused expression creep over his face as if he were a man recovering from a daze, and the light fade from his eyes. Then his face was set in the familiar stern lines, his eyes were remote, his body next to hers stiff and correct.

"I did not mean to take a liberty," he said formally. "But you are quite right, of course. Please accept my apology."

No, she wanted to cry, *call me Annabelle! That is only what I meant to say. Call me Annabelle and not Lucretia! For it is Annabelle who loves you . . .*

Caroline was coming toward them, her delicate laughter floating on the breeze. Bertram followed, carrying an armful of wood. Devon stood to meet them, and she knew she had lost him—because for only that moment she had allowed herself to forget that he must not know what she could not confess.

She could not afford the luxury of being only Annabelle.

And then he turned to her, looking at her through a mask of severity which might have hidden pain, speaking to her as though from a great distance. "You have all the powers of a fascinating woman, Miss Arnsworth," he said quietly. "Twice I have allowed you to make me forget myself. I promise you it will not happen again."

He turned away to help Bertram with the fire, leaving Annabelle with her own desolation. Was that what she held for him, then—only the fascination of a woman, like Lucretia . . . or like Caroline?

But through the remorse-filled weeks that followed, as she reviewed every moment of that poignant morning in her mind, she found one thing to hold on to, one thing which might promise that, no matter how desperate the situation appeared, perhaps all was not lost. It was the look on his face when he had thought she was hurt. It was the fear in his eyes, the intensity which flowed through his hands as he held her, the relief to find her unharmed. It suggested that perhaps he did care a little, after all.

CHAPTER 8

Annabelle's ankle, no more than mildly strained, actually healed quite quickly, but she used it as an excuse to stay home from the gatherings at which she might meet either Devon or Bertram and put the time to use by finishing up her novel. She had a stream of polite and curious callers, and Lady Marbrough allowed her to use the morning room so that she might prop her foot up on a hassock and be presentable enough to receive them. Bertram called twice, apparently in the confidence that mitigating circumstances might persuade Lady Marbrough to bend her rule and allow him to offer cheer to the bedridden. On both occasions he was told Annabelle was resting and sent away without ceremony. On the second, however, he left a box of expensive chocolates with the note: "You cannot keep to your bed forever, Miss Arnsworth, and my heart is a patient one." Annabelle deposited the note in the waste-paper box and gave the chocolates to a serving girl.

Caroline came one day with her usual stream of non-stop chatter, but as her conversation centered mostly about Devon, Annabelle found her visit more depressing than cheering. Devon had taken her driving the day before and they had stopped at a darling little tea shop and shared a confection. Devon had sat beside her at

Lady Sylveston's musicale and had kept up such a stream of amusing *sotto voce* anecdotes in counterpoint to the violins that she had feared she would positively burst a stitch to keep from laughing. Devon had done this and Devon had said that, and her papa called him a man after his own heart . . .

"For heaven's sake, Caro," exclaimed Annabelle irritably after almost half an hour of this, "does not the esteemed Mr. Lanson ever do anything which is not amusing, exciting, or fascinating? And hasn't he anything else to occupy his time but following you about like a puppy on a lead?"

Caroline drew herself up with injured dignity and replied huffily, "Well, I do say!"

"I'm sorry, Caroline," apologized Annabelle miserably. "It must be this dreadful confinement, and perhaps my ankle is beginning to ache . . ."

Caroline's expression immediately changed to one of assumed sympathy, and she soothed, "Oh, you poor dear!" as she propped up Annabelle's ankle with another cushion and made a great fuss over straightening the blanket which covered her knees. Feeling that Annabelle had atoned for her irritable outburst, Caroline sat back with a satisfied smile and declared, "There? Isn't that much better?"

"Much," murmured Annabelle, ruefully regarding the limb which was protruding at an uncomfortable angle before her.

"Do you know," said Caroline, lowering her voice with the delight at a confidence about to be shared, "Papa has made inquiries, and it turns out that perhaps

Mr. Lanson's state is not so dreary as we all have supposed."

Annabelle tried to sound interested but not convinced; polite but not inviting. "Oh?"

"Yes," she continued happily. "It seems this uncle of his—quite a recluse, it is said, and perhaps a bit dotty in the head—at any rate, it seems the uncle is the last male in direct line of descent except for a brother, who went off to America somewhere and is presumed dead without heirs, and if he *is*—dead, that is—Devon will not be entirely fortuneless when the old man passes."

Annabelle lifted an eyebrow coolly. So it was "Devon" now. "Most likely," she replied, "the brother is quite alive and well, which is why the good Mr. Lanson has made nothing of his expectations."

"Well, at any rate," insisted Caroline, "from *him* all will pass to Devon as the last male. Of course," she added, with only a slight furrow of disturbance creasing her brow, "there is not much to speak of in the manner of the estate and no solid assets at all, but it is quite different, don't you think, from an alliance with a gentleman who has nothing at *all* to his name, a virtual orphan?"

Annabelle bit back a bitter smile. "I'm quite sure."

Caroline dismissed the whole matter gaily. "Not that it would make one iota of difference to me where his family home was, for I should never live anywhere but London. I find the country *so* depressing! It is convenient, I suppose, to be listed in the Register as maintaining a country estate, but who would actually dream of living there, year around?"

"Indeed, who?" murmured Annabelle, seething inside.

And Devon came to visit, two days later. Annabelle wondered if he did not make this call, tardy though it was, only at his aunt's insistence.

She was working at the little secretaire which Lady Marbrough had thoughtfully drawn up before the window for her, and when he was announced she was so startled that she dropped several sheets of manuscript onto the floor. For a moment their gazes only interlocked, his grave, hers flustered and suspended. Then Lady Marbrough said cheerfully, "I will just take my needlework over to this window here and leave you two for a nice chat. What do you think of this particular shade of violet, Lucretia?"

Flustered, Annabelle dragged her eyes away from his to reply automatically, "It is one of my favorites."

Satisfied, Lady Marbrough took up her seat across the room and left them alone.

Devon stepped forward to retrieve the spilled papers and commented, "That appears to be quite a letter you are writing."

"It—it's my journal," replied Annabelle. "No, please, I can reach them . . ."

"Allow me." Their hands met over a single sheet of paper, and then their eyes, sharing another one of those brief, breathless, exquisitely poignant moment of things unsaid. Then Annabelle nervously retrieved the papers and he straightened up.

"It must be quite an entertaining document," he remarked. "I know of few people who use quotation marks in their private reminiscences."

"I—do like to entertain myself with my little scribblings," she replied, blushing furiously as she stuffed the papers into a drawer. "It passes the time."

He drew up a chair close to her and sat down, his face solemn, only looking at her for a time, and she thought the vibrant currents in the air would soon snap out loud if the silence were not broken. Then he said, "I would have come sooner, but I was given to understand your indisposition was of a minor nature and that you would soon be up and around. I cannot say how distressed I am to find the situation otherwise."

Again she blushed, for she knew the concern in his face was genuine, bringing back with a sharp stab of sweet remembrance the stark fear in his eyes on their last meeting when his only thought had been for her safety. She demurred, "I fear I am making rather much of it. I find I enjoy the opportunity to recuperate after my first hectic weeks here."

"Nonetheless," he insisted, "I should have come sooner."

She felt her heart would burst with emotion if she had to look another moment into those tender, sad-soft eyes, and she lifted her chin and painted a cool, sweet smile on her lips. "Indeed, Mr. Lanson," she replied, "I am surprised that you have found time to come at all. I understand the round of festivities has kept you quite busy of late."

In response, his gentle expression faded into his more natural, coolly arrogant one. "Do you indeed, Miss Arnsworth?"

"Oh, yes," she replied airily. "My callers are quite full of gossip about you. I believe you might well be taken for the talk of the town. Why"—she laughed lightly and negligently—"I believe it has gotten to the point that thoughtful Papas are making discreet inquiries into the state of your affairs."

"Now *that*," he drawled, leaning back and crossing his intriguingly muscled legs casually, "impresses me. What have they discovered?"

She lifted her shoulders negligently. "Mostly that you appear to be the sole heir to your uncle's estate and not much more."

He laughed softly, his eyes dancing in the sunlight with fascinating sparks of blue and green. "Even if that were the case," he replied, "I am certain they will be disappointed to discover that my alleged inheritance would consist only of debts, heartaches, and promises. Hardly enough to qualify me for the marriage market."

"Nonetheless," she answered cruelly, "should you make the right match, it could very easily do away with the debts and promises."

The mirth faded abruptly. "But not the heartaches."

She continued, a bit more cautiously, "And perhaps the benefits would outweigh the heartaches."

His face was stern again, his eyes far away. He answered curtly, "I have thought of that."

And then, almost before Annabelle's disappointment could register with that cold thump of alarm in the pit of her stomach, he recovered himself quickly and turned back to her. "So, Miss Arnsworth," he said conversationally, "your present misfortune aside, how are you enjoying your first social season?"

She glanced at Lady Marbrough, who was quite occupied in her own affairs with a tangled skein of thread, and answered honestly, "I sometimes become homesick."

He tipped his head acquiescently. "That is only to be expected, of course. You will soon get out of it. And only think, Brighton is but a minuscule representation of the much grander social scene in London, to which you will surely be traveling next year. You must find it all quite heady."

Now she laughed. "You mistake me, sir. I have no desire to join the social whirl in London, next year or any year. This has been a pleasurable holiday, but I will be glad to return home and take up my quiet country life again."

Now he looked interested. "Can this be true? What could your father's estate possibly have to compare with the glitter and glamour of the city?"

She looked at him for a moment, then shyly away again. "I think perhaps you could best answer that, sir. Some of us were born to social position, others to a simpler life." When he did not answer, she brought her eyes back to him defensively. "You said yourself you were more at home riding the acres than on a ballroom floor. Is it so incredible to imagine that I might feel the same way?"

"Incredible, no," he murmured, and his eyes held a strange and indecipherable look. "I have said before, you will never cease to shock me." Then, firmly, "But there can be no question of a comparison between your home and mine. While I am certain my uncle's ancestral home was a manor beyond compare in its grandeur, many lean years have seen it fall into a state of abominable disrepair. The tile is crumbling and the roof leaks and most of the rooms are boarded up. My uncle and I, in fact, share an apartment of three rooms and maintain only a single servant who balances the duties of cooking and housekeeping rather poorly. The acres, though rich, are greatly overgrown because we cannot afford to work them. There are no tenants, and if there were, most of them would probably live better than we do." He fastened her with a challenging look. "And therein," he said firmly, "lie my expectations."

She smiled tolerantly. "Are you attempting to shock *me*, Mr. Lanson?"

"Not at all," he replied steadily. "I simply hoped this description would discourage you from putting too much weight on idle gossip."

Still she pursued softly, "Yet, uncomfortable as you would have it to be, you would happily live out the rest of your life there."

Now he avoided her eyes. "It is my firmest intention," he replied quietly. "I could not be content anywhere else. Not," he added, turning back to her, "that I enjoy such a miserly existence. I assure you I am not so low-minded. If it were possible, my greatest joy would be to see the manor restored to its former splendor and the acres producing again, but"—the set of his jaw became stubborn—"since that is not to be, I shall be content to merely do the best I can with what I have. So you see, Miss Arnsworth," he said, and the expression in his eyes was very much like defiant anger, "why I cannot afford the luxury of a social butterfly for a wife whose sole thoughts revolve around how many invitations she can accumulate and how she can make her next court dress more extravagant than the last."

Annabelle drew herself up, insulted and more deeply hurt than she would allow him to know. For if he knew how gravely he had mistaken her, all would be lost . . . as though it were not already. She said coldly, "Then perhaps you had best convey that message to Miss Caroline Beckett, who appears to have thoughts upon the matter which are quite contrary to yours."

He scowled. "Miss Beckett's thoughts do not concern me."

She turned to gaze out desolately over the summer garden. No, she thought, but perhaps Caroline's fortune does. Perhaps her fortune and her very simple-mindedness could hold great appeal. Only a fool could fail to see the convenience of a match such as theirs, into which Caroline brought the means to fulfill Devon's fondest dream and the advantage of a flighty nature . . . She would be at home amid the gay whirl of the London *ton* while he remained ultimately content and undemanding in North Kent. And whatever else he may be, Devon was no fool.

Determinedly, Annabelle made a valiant effort to push Devon out of her mind and for the next few days she threw all of her energies into completing her book. It was amusing, tender, and cynical, peopled with such characters as the ever-correct Lady Marbrough, the flibbertigibbet Caroline, shy Arnold, and censorious Mrs. Wesley. No character resembled Devon Lanson. Her feelings for him were too intense to be contained within the pages of a manuscript.

With a sense of satisfaction which was the only comfort she could find to soothe her mangled spirits, she bundled up the manuscript and walked to the post office to mail it. With her urgent mission completed, she enjoyed a leisurely stroll in the warm sunshine on the way back home, nodding to acquaintances, stopping to accept compliments on her regained well-being, pausing to exchange pleasantries with matrons and young girls. And it was not long before she heard a familiar hail, "Lucretia! Oh, Lucretia!"

It was Caroline, riding in a high-perch phaeton with yellow-spoked wheels which all the town recognized as belonging to Bertram Dosset. And of course he was beside her, reining in his restless team as he swept off his hat in a low bow. "Good afternoon, Miss Arnsworth! How delightful it is to see you up and about!"

She returned the greetings and approached the dangerous-looking vehicle cautiously. The irritable back-

and-forth motions of the energetic team kept it in a constant sway and she was careful not to step too close.

"Oh Lucretia, isn't it the most exciting thing?" cried Caroline. "Now tell me quickly, for Bertie will have my head if we keep his horses standing, what does Lady Marbrough say? My mama was never so shocked—why, she had me fetch the swoon bottle! But I persuaded her it was all in good fun, though I know she will never agree if Lady Marbrough will not allow you to go—so do tell me!"

Annabelle stared at her in total bewilderment. "I'm afraid I have no idea—"

Bertram laughed softly. "It is quite possible, dear Caro, for the cards only went out today. Pray, try to be more lucid and quickly, for I shall be forced to take Miss Arnsworth up if you keep my team standing much longer."

"Bertie's ball," explained Caroline impatiently. "The masque ball! On August twenty-eighth! Did you not receive your invitation?"

"I—haven't had an opportunity to go through my cards today," replied Annabelle, somewhat at a loss, and then her eyes happened to fall upon Bertram's. They were watching her with the alert hunger of a cat at a mousehole.

"Oh, but isn't it the most deliciously scandalous thing?" went on Caroline enthusiastically. "Though of course, as I attempted to explain to Mama, it is all quite innocent and not as though it were at the home of a perfect stranger or someone not of our set, but she can be so improbably stubborn sometimes . . ."

"Please assure your chaperone, Miss Arnsworth," put in Bertram mildly, "that it is intended only as light relief to the tedium of the summer season and will be in every way in keeping with proper convention. I do most particularly desire your presence," he added with an unpleasant smile, "as it was yourself, you may recall, who so delightfully inspired the notion."

Caroline allowed a brief frown of puzzlement to distract her from the excitement at hand. "I do not recall Lucretia's ever suggesting it. How could she inspire . . . ?"

"I do beg your pardon, ladies," Bertram cut her off smoothly, "but unless Miss Arnsworth would like to come up I am very much afraid you will have to postpone your conversation to a later date."

"No." Annabelle backed away from the wheels. "You mustn't keep your horses standing any longer."

"I will call on you tomorrow!" Caroline cried gaily as the phaeton lurched off. "Do try to persuade her!"

Throughout the town that afternoon worthy matrons and anxious chaperones were putting their heads together over the problem, and none of them were able to come up with a firm decision. Eager sons and daughters argued that it promised to be only the greatest of fun and nothing improper at all; it was not as though it involved costuming, after all, only *papier-mâché* masques and dominoes which would be removed at the stroke of midnight simply for the lark, and wasn't a great ado being made about nothing, after all? Mamas conferred worriedly over the rumors of scandal and immoral conduct supposedly generated at just such affairs in London and at the French court, conceding that if the idea had been brought forth by a respected hostess perhaps it could not be regarded with such suspicion, but in the case of a bachelor, and Bertram Dosset most especially, one could not help but imagine the worst.

"I do not know, Lucretia," pondered Lady Marbrough out loud, the faintest trace of a concerned frown on her brow. "I simply do not know. Such dreadful things are said of masque balls—the idea was conceived by the French, so you can well imagine the impropriety attached!—and it has always been my contention that young people, if not constantly reminded of their conduct by the standards of dress and manners which govern a polite gathering, are far too apt to forget themselves in the spirit of the moment. I should dread to think that your dear mother would hear of it and not approve." She shook her head a little with decision. "I really believe, my dear, if it will not distress you too much, it might be for the best if you sent your regrets to Mr. Dosset. One cannot but remember his impertinence toward you at the outset, and—well, I do believe it will be for the best."

Annabelle tried to disguise her relief. "It will not distress me in the least, madam. I will go this moment to address a note to him."

"Oh, that does remind me!" Lady Marbrough went over to the desk. "In all the upset today I quite forgot. You received a letter from home."

Annabelle noticed Lucretia's neat penmanship and the line "Miss Lucretia Arnsworth, in Residence with Lady Marbrough . . ." and she could not help smiling a little with satisfaction. So far, Lucy was true to her word and watching her step. Perhaps Annabelle could rest easy in the knowledge that, if there were a mistake, it would not be at Lucretia's end.

"Thank you, Lady Marbrough," she replied. "If you will excuse me, I will take this upstairs and respond to it at the same time I reply to Mr. Dosset's invitation."

In her room, she sank to the chair by the window and prepared to read Lucy's latest news in a leisurely manner, savoring words from home.

"Annabelle, dearest!—The most wonderful thing—the most positively wonderful thing, and you have already guessed, have you not! Freddy put me to the question! He did, Annabelle, at the ball, just as I expected, and oh, my darling, what would I have done without you! It was positively the most perfect proposal any girl could have imagined, although he waited so long to do it I thought I would *despair* of him! It was the supper dance, and it was, in fact, rather warm, and I did believe he was only taking me onto the terrace for a breath of air—I actually did! And, oh, it was a lovely night, you recall how the hyacinths bloom along the border of the terrace and the trailing ivy hangs down overhead and the moon was positively *brilliant*—it was the most beautiful moon I can ever recall in all of my days. And then, Annabelle (oh, I blush with excitement even to recall it!), he suddenly grasped both my hands so severely I thought my fingers would crack!—and, Annabelle, he actually got down on one knee before me! Well, you can imagine I was quite taken aback, for I had not expected anything so passionate as this!—and

for a moment I did not know what to think. I looked at
Freddy's face and it was so distressed, so anxious and
peculiar-looking (for you know that Freddy is usually a
most composed young gentleman) that I was quite
alarmed, thinking he might be ill, and then he blurted—
I shall never forget those beautiful words!—'Miss Arnsworth, I have known you for quite some time and my
admiration and respect for you has increased to such
proportions day by day that I can no longer contain myself. Will you do me the honor of becoming my wife?'
And Annabelle, I was so *moved*, and relieved, and—yes,
surprised!—that I burst into tears! Can you imagine?
The happiest moment of my life, and I was weeping like
a schoolgirl who has lost her kitten! Well, after that was
a great deal of confusion, for my action quite distressed
Freddy until I could contain myself well enough to explain to him that it was only that I was so happy . . .
His mother and father came out and the long and short
of it is that our engagement was announced at supper,
before that of Lowrey and Chloe, naturally!"

Annabelle paused in her reading and smiled, imagin-
ing Lucretia in her ecstasy of romance, totally enraptured with her passionate young gentleman, who was, in
fact, now her fiancé. A great satisfaction stole over Annabelle, but she was not without a sense of heaviness.
So, it was accomplished. Her presence here had brought
about what it had intended to do, and now Lucy was to
be married to the man of her dreams, moving forward
into a future bright with promise. And what of Annabelle, the poor relation? Back to her flighty aunt and
her ink-stained fingers and uneventful spinsterhood,

with only memories to comfort her. Memories of a young man with tousled chestnut hair and sparkling blue-green eyes . . .

Sternly, she jerked herself out of this self-indulgent mood and read on.

"And, do you know, Bella, Mama is taking it quite better than I ever imagined. I was prepared for a great fuss, for I believed she had not always liked Freddy, but in fact she learned of it very placidly and with a positive show of good will! Do you know, I believe she was relieved to have my future settled? And of course the fact that we will be so close cannot hurt, either. Already she has sent away for linens and silk thread to begin my embroidery (although my hope chest is so full now I do not know when I shall ever have the opportunity to use it all!) and she says I may go to *London* to have my gowns made! Oh, it is all too, too, exciting, and dearest, though I would not in any means wish you to cut short your holiday I simply cannot wait for you to return, for there is so much to plan and do! Of course you will stand up for me, and we will have your gown made by the same dressmaker who does mine and who, Mama assures me, is only the very finest couturiere in all the kingdom!

"Of course it will be a June wedding, but Freddy plans to post the announcement in the *Gazette* when he goes up to London in a fortnight . . ."

Here Annabelle stopped cold, and read again. Alarm surged through her and caused her to leap to her feet, the letter falling unnoticed to the floor. An announcement in the *Gazette!* With all the world reading that Lucretia Arnsworth, while staying with Lady Marbrough in Brighton, had somehow managed at the same time to spend her summer at her country home and become engaged to a local gentleman, at whose home she was present when said engagement was announced . . . Oh, horror of horrors! How *could* they have managed to overlook this, the most dreadful of details!

Her courage failed her when she thought of Lady Marbrough, calmly unfolding the *Gazette* onto her breakfast tray, turning to the social announcements . . . And her aunt! When she learned of this, it would likely put her into a state from which she would never recover. But worse, what would happen to Lucretia's wedding plans when she found herself in the midst of a scandal which no right-thinking mama or papa would countenance . . .

Quickly, she scrambled through her writing case for pen and paper and scrawled hastily, "My dear Lucy— Please do not think me unmindful of your great joy and my own upon reading your news, but my distress over the matter which has only just come to my notice causes me to write hastily, *begging* you to dissuade Freddy from posting the announcement of your engagement before I am come home! My dear, you cannot have thought! Everyone will read that you were actually in the country when you were supposed to be in Brighton, the whole dreadful deception will come out, bringing not only great embarrassment upon myself and Lady Marbrough, but *extreme* disgrace upon you and Freddy's family. Why, you will be the laughing stock of the kingdom and your reputation ruined! And, though I am quite assured of Freddy's devotion to you, you cannot fail to see that his family would never permit a marriage steeped in such scandal, and I am equally sure that you would not wish to bring disgrace upon Freddy's head in this manner. The possibilities which arise when I think of our 'harmless deception' being uncovered in this way positively make me shudder.

"I do bemoan the day we ever put our heads together over this charade, and more deeply than you can know, but I am persuaded we shall muddle through somehow if only you can dissuade Freddy from posting the announcement so soon! No one must guess that Lucretia Arnsworth did not spend the summer in Brighton with Lady Marbrough as she was meant to be, at least not until after you are safely married and have given Freddy an heir or two.

"Please do not think me harsh, as I am as thrilled with your good fortune as I could possibly be, but only wish to urge you to do nothing which would spoil it now. I am anxious, as well, to be home and in the midst of all these splendid preparations, and I think the best thing for me to do is to take my leave of Lady Marbrough as soon as I gracefully can, but I do not see how this can possibly be arranged before the first of August.

"We will spend hours talking when I return home, meanwhile only write your reassurance to me immediately. I remain as ever your loving cousin, Annabelle."

She quickly folded and sealed the letter and gathered up her bonnet and gloves to go out. And trailing in her very steps with a dogged persistence were Sir Walter Scott's lines that her aunt was fond of repeating: "Oh, what a tangled web we weave, when first we practice to deceive."

Never had any solid truth been more unwelcome.

CHAPTER 9

The afternoon sun was low in the sky by the time she stepped outside to make her second journey of the day to the post office—she knew that if she hurried she would be able to send her urgent missive by the last coach. And hurry she did, her head down, her eyes upon her steps, her skirts swinging briskly about her ankles with a stride that Lady Marbrough would be certain to consider most unladylike.

Immediately after she returned to the house, she must approach Lady Marbrough about an early departure. Her hostess would be most distressed and probably put forth great resistance, and Annabelle did not look forward to the interview. Lady Marbrough had invited her here, after all, with every certainty that she would leave affianced to her nephew, and so far very little progress had been made in that direction. It was a thought which clutched tearfully at Annabelle's throat and she had to struggle valiantly to dismiss it from her mind. No one would have been happier to see Lady Marbrough's expectations fulfilled than Annabelle herself, but it was impossible, it had been impossible from the start, and every moment she lingered only prolonged the pain. If Devon ever learned her true identity he would despise her, not only for the deception, but for her profession, which epitomized all he held in distaste between the slim covers of a volume entitled *Patches and Pins*. And Annabelle Morgan could bring him none of the advantages of name and wealth that Lucretia Arnsworth could. Even with those supposed advantages, he managed to keep his cool distance. How could she ever imagine that, stripped of name and fortune down to simple Annabelle Morgan, poor relation, his attitude toward her would in any way change for the better? No, it was a hopeless situation, and she must not ponder it—only be well out of it as quickly as possible.

She had been a fool to ever have allowed her heart to lead her so astray, and now she must pay for it. Now that Lucy was safely engaged, Annabelle's presence was no longer required here. It could, in fact, serve only to jeopardize what had already been accomplished. So she must leave all of this behind her, get on with the business of living her own life, and somehow, in some manner yet unknown to her, discover a way to begin forgetting about Devon Lanson.

So intent was she on her direction, so totally absorbed in her own tragic thoughts, that it was inevitable that she would eventually walk directly into something or someone . . . and it was to her great misfortune that the someone happened to be Bertram Dosset.

"Why, my dear Miss Arnsworth!" he cried, catching her shoulders to steady her. "I do say, are you quite all right?"

"Yes," she replied breathlessly, flustered. She had dropped her letter and she stooped to retrieve it. "I'm terrible sorry . . ."

"No, indeed, my fault entirely. Do allow me . . ." His hand reached the letter before hers, and to her horror the first line of the address glared up at her, "To Miss Lucretia Arnsworth . . ." Her heart seemed to stop for as much as two beats before resuming its slow, painfully laborious thudding again.

It seemed he stared at it for a long time. When at last he looked at her, his lip was curved upward in a cold, mirthless half-smile, and his eyes were as deadly as a blade. "Why," he remarked smoothly, "it is a fortunate thing that you did not post this. It seems you have accidently addressed it to yourself."

"How silly of me." Hastily she retrieved it without looking at him. How could she have been so foolish? In her haste it had been she who had made the mistake, after all of her concern over Lucy. "I was in a great hurry . . ." she floundered, feeling herself sinking deeper and deeper into inextricable mire.

"I could not help but notice." With confident insolence, he tucked her arm securely through his and resumed his leisurely stroll down the street. "It is a great pity when we allow ourselves to be swept into too much of a rush . . . so many of life's little pleasures are missed."

She made a small effort to free her arm, not desiring to cause a scene on the street. "Indeed, Mr. Dosset, but as it happens today I am in rather of a hurry . . ."

He glanced at her with an unpleasant quirk of the eyebrow which sent a shiver up her spine. "Ah, yes," he said softly, "to post the misdirected letter, of course. Nonetheless, surely you can spare a few moments to stroll with me. We have had so little chance to become acquainted, and I promise I will not detain you."

Annabelle stiffened with a forced courage and replied coolly, "Perhaps a few moments."

"So," he continued with that irksome pleasantness, "I am most anxious to know—will you be attending my ball?"

Now she could almost relax. At least her present situation indicated that that was *one* crisis she would not have to face. "I am very much afraid not, Mr. Dosset," she replied. "As it happens, my plans will see me home before the date of your ball."

If she expected a more violent reaction from him, she was to be disappointed. "But that would be most unfortunate, Miss Arnsworth," he protested mildly. "Your presence at my little affair is quite imperative."

"As I said, Mr. Dosset, it will be impossible . . ."

"Nothing," he assured her, "is all *that* impossible." He glanced at her with an intimate smile which made her blood run cold. "I would have thought, as a matter of fact, that the theme of the ball would have given you quite a bit of pleasure. You do enjoy masquerades, do you not?"

She swallowed hard and said nothing.

"Now surely," he continued, "you can postpone your plans for a few days and manage to be present. There was a matter of most particular importance I had wished to discuss with you on that occasion."

The bright July sun suddenly ducked behind a tree and it seemed in that moment Annabelle's entire future was similarly eclipsed. She said, "I am sure that any matter of such importance can be discussed now and need not wait for the ball."

He laughed softly, shaking his head. "I am impossibly sentimental over such things as atmosphere and timing. You must indulge me."

"I am afraid that is quite impossible," she managed. "Even if I were to change my plans, my chaperone has already informed me that she does not approve of your ball and will not allow me to attend."

"Oh, but you are such a persuasive young lady," he assured her smoothly. "I cannot imagine anyone refusing you anything you had your heart quite set on. Lady Marbrough will change her mind if you ask her to do so."

The worst was, Annabelle knew it was true. She had no reply.

To her silence, he added in a moment, very casually, "Oh, by the by, I had a letter the other day which might interest you. From my cousin Lowrey." Her heart jerked and then resumed its thunderous antics in the region of her throat. "He writes of a most interesting chat with your mother the other day." Now he bent a glance on her and there was no mistaking the deadly purpose in his eyes. "It was an altogether rather peculiar letter at that," he mused. "Yes, extremely peculiar."

Again, Annabelle could not find her voice.

"As a matter of fact," he continued thoughtfully, "it has put me in mind of a most interesting notion. If you find yourself unable to change your plans or to persuade Lady Marbrough to allow you to attend my ball, perhaps it would serve if I rode out and paid your mother a call. I am certain that, once I told her what a delightful time you were having here, she would not dream of cutting your stay short. And if I should happen to mention in passing my little party—I am quite sure her permission would override Lady Marbrough's objections."

Annabelle shivered even as a breeze parted the branches of the tree to allow the last dying rays of day to fall warm upon her shoulders. She had no doubt but that he meant it. Perhaps this had been his intention all along, to torture her with anxiety until the exactly proper moment presented itself for her exposure . . . and she knew with a deadly dread that he had planned that moment for the night of the masque ball.

But to what purpose? What benefit could he possibly obtain by humiliating her, shocking Lady Marbrough, and dragging Lucy into scandal? This totally perplexed her and was, at any rate, of no moment. What she needed now was time, and if she flew in his face at this moment, she had no doubt but that within the hour he would be racing his phaeton out of town toward her aunt's residence, and she could not do that to Lucy. She simply could not.

She said, her voice strained with the effort, "I am quite sure that will not be necessary, Mr. Dosset. I see no reason to involve those at home in my personal affairs while I am on holiday."

He smiled in quiet victory. "And will I see you at my ball?"

She replied steadily, "You may count upon it."

"Ah, lovely." And suddenly he stopped, releasing her arm. "And here we are, just in time for the evening post.

I will take my leave of you . . ." His eyes raked her up and down with a familiarity which made her flesh crawl as he swept her a bow, "Until next we meet."

He turned to go, and Annabelle felt herself begin to shiver all over, perhaps with the aftereffects of shock, perhaps with relief at his absence. And then, horribly, he turned back to her. "Oh, by the by," he added casually, and the smooth lack of expression on his face could have been molded by the devil himself, "when next you hear from her . . . do give my best to the lovely Miss Arnsworth."

He crossed the street in a smooth, graceful pace, looking neither right nor left, and Annabelle had to reach out a hand to brace herself to keep from sinking weakly against the building.

That night, as Lady Marbrough sat with her needlepoint and Annabelle held a book stiffly in her lap on one of their few evenings at home, she found an opportunity to broach the subject gently.

"You look a bit pale this evening, my dear," commented Lady Marbrough. "I do hope you did not overdo on your first day about."

"As a matter of fact," began Annabelle cautiously, closing the unread book, "I have been seized by a notion which I simply cannot get out of my head, and it rather distresses me."

Lady Marbrough looked up, her attention captured. "Oh, dear. And what might that be?"

"Only"—Annabelle looked down, her fingers nervously toying with the edges of the pages—"only how often we are hasty in passing judgment on others, and how unpleasantly that judgment might affect the lives of persons to whom we never intended any real harm."

A small perplexity crossed Lady Marbrough's brow. "I am afraid I do not understand, my dear."

"Mr. Bertram Dosset, for example," continued Annabelle, still unable to raise her eyes. "Has it not occurred to you that perhaps we have been a bit harsh with him, when in fact he has given us no good reason at all?"

Lady Marbrough hesitated. "It is true," she admitted reluctantly, "that he has always been quite courteous to me. And, except for that one error in judgment at the outset—which we cannot be entirely certain was his fault—he has shown only the utmost respect for you, my dear. But the fact remains his reputation leaves much to be desired . . ."

"I am very much afraid," put in Annabelle, "that a person would have no chance at all to reform if well-meaning citizens like you and me refused to allow him an opportunity to overcome his reputation."

Lady Marbrough seemed to consider this in silence for a time. "What are you suggesting?"

"It is only," answered Annabelle, and at last was able to look her hostess in the eye, "that I was thinking of his ball. You realize, ma'am, that when word gets around that you will not allow me to attend, all of the ladies will withhold their permission for their young people to attend and he will be forced to cancel the affair. It will be most humiliating for him. It will, in fact, amount to no less than a direct cut from all polite society in Brighton, and I doubt that his reputation, already, as you have pointed out, besmirched, could ever recover from such a blow. Soon he would not be received in London, and as word traveled, there would not be a respectable home in the country in which he was welcome. He might even have to retire to the Continent . . ." She shook her head sadly. "I would hate to have that on my conscience."

Lady Marbrough managed to smile through an anxious frown which betrayed her doubt. "I am sure it could not be *that* serious. However," she added thoughtfully, "if no one came to his ball—and I am persuaded you are quite right in your assumption that our refusal would only pave the way for others—it would be quite a cut, would it not? And I cannot think that the gentleman has done anything so wrong as to deserve that."

Annabelle fought back a bitter smile. *If only you knew, Lady Marbrough,* she thought. And soon she would. But not until Annabelle had discovered some way to protect Lucretia, to deliver them both from this awful tangle . . .

"Perhaps," ventured Lady Marbrough, "I should reconsider."

"That would be most generous of you," murmured Annabelle, though her heart sank like a stone to her feet.

By the time Annabelle and Lady Marbrough completed their round of calls the next day, every reluctant or undecided mama in Brighton had decided to follow the trustworthy Lady Marbrough's lead, and every son and daughter was in an ecstasy of excitement.

"I knew it, I just knew it," squealed Caro, smothering

Annabelle with an embrace. "Oh, won't it be just the most *titillating* thing? I can hardly wait, can you?"

Annabelle was hard put to return even a small smile. For her, it was only the postponement of the day of execution. Her only hope lay in her own wits, with the minute possibility that she would discover some way to forestall Bertram before the event brought their separate wills to the test.

"Mr. Lanson is in the parlor," announced Braddock perfunctorily when at last they returned home.

Lady Marbrough lifted her eyebrows in mild surprise. "Now I wonder what he can be doing here? He knows this is not my regular at-home day."

"He was in quite a temper when he came, that he was," volunteered Braddock as she took their gloves and capes. "But I've had him cooling his heels for nigh onto an hour now, so I'll wager he's forgot what it was he came for by now!"

Lady Marbrough responded, "Oh, very well. Do go in and speak to him, Lucretia, while I refresh my face with lemon water. I declare, this heat is insufferable."

But as it happened, Braddock's prediction about his softened temper did not turn out to be correct. He was pacing back and forth before the window, his hands clasped tightly behind his back, and when Annabelle came in he whirled on her.

"Where have you been?" he demanded.

She was taken aback. "Really, Mr. Lanson, I see no call for you to address me in that tone! As you surely must know, this is our day for making calls—"

He waved his hand impatiently. "I've no time now for

that nonsense. Tell me now, is it true? I said I would not believe it until I heard it from your own lips—is it true?"

A flood of guilt poured through Annabelle's veins, weakening her limbs so that she found she must sit. She had been discovered! Bertram had told him, and—she had been discovered!

"Is—what true?" she managed, swallowing hard. "I'm afraid I don't—"

"The masque ball," he returned curtly, his eyes dark with fury. "You have decided to accept the invitation."

Wonderful relief flowed through her, bringing new life to her numbed senses and color to her cheeks. "Why, yes," she admitted, "that is correct. As a matter of fact—"

"You even went so far," he interrupted harshly, "as to *beg* my aunt for permission—"

Now she bristled. "I did not beg," she said.

"My aunt would never have given her consent to such a contemptible undertaking had you not used every device at your disposal . . ." He broke off with an angry breath and turned abruptly away. "I should have known," he muttered fiercely, with his back to her. "I should have known it yesterday when I saw the two of you with your heads together as bold as brass in broad daylight and in the middle of the street—"

Annabelle said cautiously, "You—saw us?"

"Yes," he spat angrily and turned. "But of course you were too enraptured with Mr. Dosset to notice me. Oh, you are quite a self-sufficient young lady, are you not, Miss Arnsworth? You will follow the first rose-strewn path you see with any gentleman who offers to take you —heedless of the advice of others whose only concern has always been your welfare. I only hope you may not find that path leads to your own destruction." He picked up his hat, tossed carelessly upon the window seat, and turned on his heel toward the door.

Annabelle half rose, alarm at his rage and his own misinterpretation of her motives urging her into protest. "Please—you mistake me! You do not understand—"

"No." The smile that he gave her was cold and mirthless and did not mitigate the injured look in his eyes. "I am sure I do not. The conduct of an heiress has always been beyond my comprehension, and I think I could not ask for more than that they should forever remain so."

Lady Marbrough entered, declaring smoothly, "Now, Devon, whatever has put you into such a—"

"I beg your pardon, madam," he interrupted coldly, his eyes upon Annabelle. "I find I cannot stay."

He pushed past his aunt with hardly more than a glance, and as she stared after him in astonishment, he suddenly turned back at the door. "I have become accustomed to being amazed by you, Miss Arnsworth," he said quietly. "Until now, the surprises were always pleasant."

Devon did not return to that house for over a week, and though her heart was filled with anxiety and her nights sleepless as she sought to unravel her own problems, the vision which returned to her mind most often during those days was the look of pain in Devon's eyes as he had left her.

On the evening of the sixth of August, the Ladies' Society for the Advancement of the Cultural Arts, of which Lady Marbrough was chairwoman, had planned a musicale featuring selections by Weber and Mozart on the piano and the dubious vocal talents of Lady Marian Carstairs *en opérette*. The function was to be held at the home of Lady Marbrough in the hopes of offsetting some of the undesirable effects that the excitement of the upcoming ball had generated. It was to be a very staid and formal affair, and Annabelle was looking forward to a quiet evening in which to gather her thoughts.

Annabelle busied herself with supervising the arrangement of chairs and the placing of potted flowers while Lady Marbrough went to select for herself the choice lobster which would be part of a light buffet. When the morning post came Annabelle spotted immediately a letter from Lucretia, and, calling a few last instructions to the servants, she took it into the morning room, where she knew she would be undisturbed.

When she opened it, another packet fell out. She saw it was from Fitzroy, Patterson & Potts, Publishers. She read Lucretia's letter first.

"My dear Bella—Please do calm yourself, for your instructions have been obeyed to the letter. I suppose I did get a bit carried away in the moment, but I beg you not to worry yourself into such an absolute dither. I merely told Freddy I was inclined to keep our engagement confined for a time to our closest friends and neighbors, hinting that Mama has not entirely adjusted to my new status, and he was most accommodating. I went on to add how very distraught I should be if he should leave me for London at this moment, so he has decided to postpone his journey until October. So you see, my dear, there is no problem at all. Honestly, Bella, sometimes you quite distress me with your predisposition to fly into the wind over trifles . . ."

Almost, Annabelle laughed out loud with relief, and she sank weakly to a chair. Trifles!

"Mama says we should not dream of asking you to cut short your stay only on the account of my engagement. It would be quite different if you were to miss the wedding, of course, but she has her obligation to Lady Marbrough and I am afraid she would be most displeased with us both should you come home early. Of course I miss you, dearest, and I have *so* much to share with you, but nothing which cannot keep another month, only this: what do you think of oyster as a shade for your gown? Perhaps trimmed with tiny little pearls about the neck and sleeves? I think the color would be positively fascinating with your dark hair and do wonders for your complexion, don't you agree?

"I have enclosed a letter from Fitzroy, Patterson & Potts—probably regarding a new order of those books you are always spending your pin money on. Of course, my dear, it is your affair, but I do believe I would take my business elsewhere could the company concerned not show more courtesy than to address me as *Mr.* A. P. Morgan.

"I am in a rush to get this in the earliest post, as you

requested, so I will write more later. I am your most devoted and *blissfully* happy, Lucy."

Annabelle hesitated and then took up the letter from the publishers.

"My dear Mr. Morgan:—Allow me to thank you for forwarding to us your latest novel, *Dougherty's Dilemma*. We found it intriguing and witty and plan to bring it out as soon as possible as the necessary sequel to *Patches and Pins*, and with every confidence of the same success.

"Enclosed please find a cheque for one hundred pounds . . ."

Annabelle found it. She detached the cheque from the letter and folded it, with Lucretia's missive, into the bosom of her gown, her mind on other things. She closed the door to the morning room and went upstairs, trying to form a reply to Lucretia in her mind.

For almost half an hour she wrestled with the decision as to whether or not to inform Lucretia of the true nature of her situation here, and the danger of imminent exposure. Little time remained until the ball and she had discovered no weapons with which to fight back against Mr. Bertram Dosset. But what good would it do to alarm Lucretia prematurely, to send her into such a state that she would undoubtably blurt out the whole thing to her mother when there still might be a chance of rescue? Besides, unless Annabelle could think of something, and quickly, Lucretia would know soon enough. Everyone would know.

At last, Annabelle sat down at her desk and began, "Dearest Lucy—Forgive me, if you will, for flying into a 'dither.' I should have known I could count upon you to put everything to rights, and thank you for handling it all so smoothly.

"I know we have scores of things to discuss and I am as anxious as you to begin. But as for oyster, though I am quite fond of oyster as a seafood I must admit it is not one of my particular favorites when it comes to shades of fabric . . ."

Neither Annabelle nor anyone else had occasion to go into the morning room during the remainder of that hectic day. And so, by the time she was dressed and downstairs receiving the guests for the musicale that evening she had completely forgotten the missive from Fitzroy, Patterson & Potts, now lying open on the desk by the window.

There was no way she could expect to avoid Bertram the entire evening, and so she steeled herself to confront him with pleasantness and brightness, with never an indication that anything was amiss.

"I wonder, Miss Arnsworth," he inquired politely, "if you would do me the great honor of allowing me to take you into the musicale when it begins?"

"I am dreadfully sorry, Mr. Dosset," she returned sweetly, "but I have promised my aunt to sit beside Mrs. Yarnel, at the back. She is dreadfully deaf, you know, and often disturbs the other listeners with her constant inquiries as to what piece is being sung or played and in what key." She gave him another melting smile. "I *do* wish you had asked earlier, however, for nothing would give me greater pleasure."

He insisted, a surprised yet gratified light in his own eyes, "Every lady has two sides, Miss Arnsworth."

"Yes, and isn't it a pity that Lady Marbrough is occupying the other?"

She turned and at just that moment her eyes fell upon Devon, standing not more than three feet away, his face molded into stone with taut disapproval, his eyes dark. He bowed to her briefly. "Miss Arnsworth," he said and moved on. She knew he had overheard every word of Bertram's invitation and her own simpering reply, and she knew what he had assumed. She knew it quite clearly and with a terrible wrenching of her heart when she saw him escort Caroline into the music room and arrange their seats in the shadows of the back row. But there was nothing, simply nothing, she could do.

There was to be an hour of Chopin, followed by the inimitable performance of Lady Marian, and after that a welcome break for the buffet. Annabelle had promised her hostess to take upon herself the responsibility of seeing that everything was in readiness at the buffet table and was happy to make her discreet exit when Lady Marian began her recital.

Lady Marbrough's servants were precise and well trained, and there was very little to oversee. The quivering lobster jelly was arranged attractively upon a silver platter at the head of the table, the refreshing lemon ice at its foot. The centerpiece of blazing roses, the cutlery, the china and crystal were all perfectly placed. She paused to arrange a bit of watercress more attractively on a platter of finger sandwiches and turned to go. She

could not help gasping a little as she saw Bertram leaning casually against the door, a lazy smile curving the
corners of his lips.

"I could not, in all respect to my poor ears, linger a
moment longer," he said.

She gave a bright litttle laugh and cast a nervous
glance over her shoulder. The servants had gone back to
the kitchen, and they were alone. "Truly, Mr. Dosset, I
cannot think you would wish that compliment to reach
Lady Marian's ears!"

He took a step forward, looking at her, his smile tightening as if he were savoring something delicious—something unpleasantly intimate and, perhaps, dangerous.
He said softly, "Lady Marian may go to the devil at this
moment for all I care."

Quickly, she made to move past him. "I really do
think we should return now. Our absence will be noticed."

He blocked her path, and his eyes began to dance
madly. "Why, Miss Arnsworth, I do believe you are
frightened of me!" he cried delightedly.

She lifted her chin coolly. "I fear no man, Mr. Dosset.
Please step aside."

But as she again made to push past him, he caught
her shoulders in a grip that made her cry out in surprise
and alarm, and he drew her close. "That is good," he
said, his eyes scanning her face, her throat, her bosom,
rapidly and hungrily. "You have no need to fear me, you
know. Your secret is safe with me, Miss—whatever-
your-name-is—because I have great plans for you. And
all it will take to bring them to fruition is your coopera-

tion . . ." He bent his face close to hers and drew her abruptly against him so tightly that his coat buttons cut into her breasts painfully.

With a cry, she wrenched away, and just then the serving door opened, admitting an underling with another tray of wine. He stepped away, his eyes dark and menacing, yet mindful of the servant. "Never mind," he said softly. "For I will have you, Miss *Arnsworth*, one way or another. And you *will* cooperate, for you have a great deal too much to lose if you do not."

Quickly she caught up her skirts and fled past him, across the corridor and into the first unoccupied room she found, the morning room. There she made it as far as the window and then stopped, shuddering with horror, bringing her hands up to cover her face and letting at last the burning tears come. What was she to do, what was she to do? *Cooperate!* Oh, the dreadful sound of that word, evoking highwaymen in the night and cutthroats and . . . oh, Lucy! she thought in despair, what have I done to you? He will have us both ruined at a moment's notice and without a flicker of regret and there is nothing I can do to prevent it . . .

"Oh," she cried out loud into her hands, "that *odious* man!"

"Lucretia."

She whirled, and it was Devon who was standing in the doorway, now crossing swiftly toward her, alarm and concern stamped on his face, and she sobbed out loud in relief. "Lucretia, what is it? What has happened? Why are you weeping?"

"Oh—Devon!" she whispered tearfully, and suddenly

she was in his arms, held tight against his chest and weeping into his shirt and his lips were light against her hair.

"Lucretia," he whispered, "my dearest—my darling—do not cry. I am here. I am here . . ."

She lifted her face to him, and the tenderness in his eyes had turned to passion, she felt his fingers tighten with a warm throb against her back and his lips were upon hers, the taste of her tears and the flood of joy mingling into the spiraling dizziness of the deep, demanding, all-encompassing delight of his kiss. His lips wandered to her face, her eyes, her ears, the pulse of her throat, and she yielded to it helplessly, each searing breath sending a jolt of fire through her veins until she thought, for the first time in her life, she surely might swoon.

"When I saw him follow you," he whispered huskily, lifting his face to search hers with eyes which were raw with hunger, "I thought I would go mad with jealousy. I thought the tryst had been prearranged . . . I was a fool to ever have thought so." And suddenly his hands tightened upon her arms with the naked strength of a man possessed and his eyes darkened with violent intensity. "But tell me now," he demanded hoarsely, "if he has done anything to harm you, for I swear I will see him on the dueling field before sunrise . . ."

"No," she whispered quickly, wanting only for the dark mood to be gone so that she might rest once more securely in his arms. "No, please, it was nothing like that . . ."

"Oh, my love!" Again her lips were in the warm, urgent clasp of his and she returned the kiss joyfully, loving his demands, wanting his passion . . . wanting it never to end. His fingers were strong and forceful against the back of her neck, shocking her with warm electric thrills wherever they touched, even though they guided her head to rest against his chest so that she could not see his eyes nor feel the wonderful pressure of his lips probing hers. His chest was rising and falling with the heaviness of his breath as the whisper of it rushed against her ear until she thought her entire body would soon go up in flames. His heart throbbed in urgent counterpoint to her own, and he whispered, "Oh, my dear, have you any idea how nearly you have come to driving me mad with desire these past weeks? I must have known from the moment I first met you that there would be no other woman for me . . . yet, not believing my good fortune, I persisted in making a fool of myself. And though I saw immediately in what contempt you held me"—she struggled to protest, but his embrace prevented her—"and I tried to forget you, each thing you did, each word you said, found me falling more desperately in love with you . . ."

She lifted her face to him, laughing and close to tears again with wild joy. "Oh, Devon, you must know that I loved you to distraction from the outset, only I did not think—"

His mouth came down upon hers again, his arms tightened about her waist so severely that she lost her breath and she knew if not for the support of those arms her knees would surely give way. When she opened her eyes again the room was swirling hotly, his lips were pressed with ever-increasing urgency against her throat, her shoulders, the little cleft between her breasts . . . She whispered breathlessly, "Devon—we must not . . . someone might come . . . I—I feel quite faint . . ."

He drew her into a final embrace. "My love," he whispered desperately, "forgive me . . . I only have contained my passion for you so long that I cannot have enough of your sweet presence. Only of course," he admitted finally and held her for a very long time, "you are right."

At length they parted, reluctantly and rather shakily, and still he held her with one hand cupped lightly about her face, his eyes soft and tender and adoring as he looked at her. Her own eyes shining, she reached for his hand and brought it gently to her lips. His fingers closed about hers.

"Do you think," he said softly, "that we might speak with my aunt?"

She could not restrain the spark of joy and excitement which leaped to her eyes, and she whispered, "When?"

He retrieved his hand, smiling. "Is this very moment too soon?"

"Oh!" She brought both hands to her hot face, delighted and flustered. "Only—give me a moment to collect myself. I am very much afraid if I confronted her like this it would take most of the surprise from our secret."

He smiled tenderly as she turned away to pin up a

straying curl, and his eyes fell upon something which had, in the intensity of the previous moments, fallen unnoticed to the floor. "It seems I am forever spilling your papers," he commented lightly and bent to retrieve it.

When Annabelle turned she was at first bewildered by the cold expression which had come over his face as he studied the paper he held in his hand, and her mouth opened to form the word "What—" And then she knew.

She froze, unable to move or speak or breathe, and she felt the color drain coldly from her cheeks and the animated expression on her face fade into one of cold silence. Still his eyes fastened upon the paper, his fingers clenched about it so tightly that its edges crumpled, and when he turned to her, extending it, his eyes were as cold and as remote as his voice. He said, "Yours?"

She simply nodded and took it from him. For a long time silence throbbed in the room, a silence as clear and ringing as their joy had been only a moment ago, and she could not look at him.

At last he said, very softly, "So, you are the infamous Mr. A. P. Morgan, lurking about polite parlors and taking delight in mocking decent folk with your pseudonymous writings. I have thought many things of you, Miss Arnsworth, but never that. I am impressed."

She lifted her eyes to him desperately. "Devon, please, let me explain . . ."

He straightened his cuff with a flick of his wrist, and the smile on his face was cold. "Thank you, I believe I will wait and read the book. I trust you have collected enough material this summer to make quite an interesting little tale." He bowed to her stiffly. "I bid you good evening."

And though her heart cried out in agony to him, his did not hear. The door closed quietly and firmly on his exit.

CHAPTER 10

A day passed, and two, and Annabelle heard nothing from Devon. She vacillated between anger, despair, and the agony of a broken heart. He had said he loved her— did he not at least owe her the opportunity to explain? And yet what would she explain? His love had not even survived the test of the discovery of her profession, a very minor thing indeed in comparison with all he must learn if their hastily confessed love were to ever have a chance.

Somehow, in the passion of the moment, she had perhaps convinced herself that he would understand and forgive. In the cold light of a bright summer's morning she knew she had expected too much. He was in love with Lucretia Arnsworth, a fascinating heiress who had ensnared him in the web of her deceit. Of Annabelle Morgan he knew nothing and doubtless never wished to know anything.

Still, some small kernel of hope prevailed, as it would in a woman blinded by love, until that fateful morning.

She came downstairs and discovered Lady Marbrough scanning a note which would effectively snuff it forever. As she read, the older woman's face became suffused with a choleric tint, the cords in her neck protruding with an emotion quite unlike anything Annabelle had ever expected to witness in that even-tempered lady, and her lips compressed so tightly they were almost white.

"Well!" she managed at last, and in a peculiar strangulated tone. "Well, I never in my life!"

"Lady Marbrough!" Annabelle moved toward her in alarm. "What is it?"

Her hostess' hands shook a little as she indicated the paper she held, and it was a gesture of pure wrath, thinly controlled. "This!" she returned, and her eyes narrowed with contempt. "Of all the ungrateful—inconsiderate—it is that wretched nephew of mine!"

Annabelle's heart lurched at the very mention of him, and she moved forward quickly. "Devon?" she inquired, trying to keep her tone steady. "What has he done?"

"He has left town, that's what he has done," Lady Marbrough returned angrily, "and without so much as a by-your-leave or a thank-you-very-much. Oh, I have known him to be inconsiderate before, brutish and haphazard. But always I thought I could count upon him to at least maintain some vestige of polite behavior—oh, this is too much! I shall never forgive him for this, no, never!"

"Does he," ventured Annabelle, swallowing hard, "does he say why?"

The other glanced scornfully at the note once more. "Some nonsense about news of his uncle. A patent excuse for inexcusable behavior designed purely to hurt me, and I shall not tolerate it, no, let me assure you of that! He may stay in that nasty old house in North Kent until he *withers* of old age before he will hear another word from me, of that you may be sure!" She crumpled up the note and strode angrily from the room.

And so, Annabelle thought disconsolately, he could not even stay another day in the same town with me, so greatly does he hold me in contempt. She knew that at last it was irretrievably over—she would never see Devon Lanson again. She thought she could bear the pain of that, that she could return home and somehow manage to weld the shattered strings of her life into a semblance of harmony again—it would not be a pain which would ever heal, a longing which would ever dissipate, but it was one with which she could learn to live. It was the thought that he would live the rest of his life believing she had used him only as another amusing character for her book, that she was scheming and fickle and totally without heart, which cut her to the core and would haunt her the rest of her days.

Though her life for her seemed at that moment to have ended, though her only thought now was to escape from this place with its bittersweet memories to the comfort of her own spartan little room in the heart of the English countryside, bolstered by Lucretia's giddy joy and her aunt's befuddled placidity, her torment was not yet over. If she even considered going home now, Bertram Dosset would be upon her aunt's doorstep ready to tell all. And though her spirits were aching and her senses shattered, she must still discover some way to save Lucy. In fact, that was the *only* thing that mattered now.

The weeks crept by in inches, and on the afternoon of the ball she was as hopeless as she had been when Bertram last approached her. The only possibility of salvation lay within that dreadful word: "cooperation." What did Bertram want from her? What could she possibly do to keep his silence?

She was restlessly trying to nap that afternoon when an unexpected visitor was announced. Annabelle got up, irritably buttoning her bodice and smoothing her hair, for it was only Caro who waited in the receiving parlor and Annabelle had counted on a few hours rest to restore her strength for the upcoming ordeal.

Caroline was perched eagerly on the edge of the divan, her hands clasped within the folds of a light summer muff, her cheeks flushed excitedly beneath the brim of a fetching blue bonnet. "Oh, Lucretia, my dear," she exclaimed, rising, "I *am* so sorry to disturb you at this hour and with the ball only *moments* away, but I simply *had* to tell you the most shocking thing!"

"I was resting," replied Annabelle, "and I would have thought you would have been too. Will you have some tea?"

Caroline shook her head impatiently. "No, I will only stay a moment, I've simply *scores* of things to do, but I couldn't get with one of them until I told *someone!*"

"Well," Annabelle responded without much interest, "what is it?"

Caroline glanced meaningfully at the door and, smothering an exasperated sigh, Annabelle closed it.

"I have only just discovered," she said in a low, excited tone, taking a step closer, "that at the ball tonight no one is to be announced!"

Annabelle looked at her in incredulity. "Is that all?"

"But my dear, don't you see?" Caroline insisted with all the delight of a naughty secret. "If no one is announced and we are all in masques, no one will have any idea who anyone else is—which leads, I am told, to the most shocking sorts of unconventional behavior because, you understand, there is no one to whom to account for it the next morning! It is precisely the way it is done at the French court!"

Annabelle sat down casually in the chair near the fireplace and almost smiled at Caroline's frivolousness. "I hardly think anyone we know would be prone to—unconventional behavior, under any circumstances."

Caroline shook her head impatiently, sitting across from her. "No, no that is not the point at *all*. It is that Bertie has kept it secret and in fact told no one but me until this very moment, and my mother would positively *swoon* if she knew anything of the sort was being considered! But don't you find it dreadfully *exciting*—I mean, it does so lend itself to intrigue and *amour caché* and all sorts of simply *scintillating* possibilities!" She giggled, and then quickly sobered. "Oh, Lucretia, you will not say anything, will you? To Lady Marbrough, I mean? It would simply be *too* dreadful—"

Annabelle smiled negligently. "I hardly think it is

worth mentioning at all. After all, the masques will be removed at midnight . . ."

"Yes, but it is simply the *idea!* So *original—*"

There was a tap at the door, and Annabelle called, "Yes?"

Braddock came in, and in her hand was a small nosegay of passion-pink rosebuds. At first Annabelle's heart did a slow, painful roll and then quickened with excitement, for swift in her memory was another nose-gay . . . But it was quite impossible.

Braddock said, "For you, miss." And Annabelle was surprised at the steadiness of her hands as she took them.

Caroline pouted, "Why, that nasty Bertie! Do you know he sent me an identical nosegay only yesterday? It shall go into the waste-paper box the moment I return home, that much is certain!"

Annabelle unfolded the card and read, "Wear these tonight if you will keep your promise." There was no signature, and Annabelle frowned. Promise? What promise . . . ?

To cooperate . . .

Annabelle said steadily, "Who brought these?"

"A street urchin, miss. Shall I put them in water?"

"No," said Annabelle stiffly and returned them to her. "You may toss them away or keep them for yourself. I will not be wearing them."

Braddock gave her a peculiar look as she took the flowers from the room, and Caroline sat back, the smug delight of a new secret lighting in her eyes. "Well!" she said softly. "That will set Bertie on his ear!" She glanced at Annabelle slyly. "He is rather sweet on you, you know."

"Is he?" responded Annabelle coolly, and Caroline tried another tactic.

"I suppose you will be going unescorted tonight."

"Since Mr. Lanson has left town," replied Annabelle evenly, "I suppose I will."

Caroline made a short dismissing gesture with her hand. "Fie on the fine Mr. Lanson!" she said. "One could have expected no better of him, I suppose."

Now Annabelle was interested. "Oh? And how is that?"

Caroline leaned forward, and the expression which widened her eyes was genuine amazement. "Have you any idea what he revealed to me when last we met? And quite in the most casual way, too! He said"—now she shuddered a little, as though the very remembrance was distasteful—"that his wife would be expected to milk cows and chop fodder and produce at least a child a year! Can you imagine? He was quite serious, too. He went on to say that he thought I would look quite fetching in the woolen homespun that is woven from his own sheep and that I would soon grow accustomed to the solitude . . . Can you just *imagine*? Well, I sent him on his way pretty quick, I can tell you that!" She sat back, folding her hands again within the muff with an air of petulant satisfaction. "Just imagine! And we had that man in our drawing room!"

Annabelle fought back unexpected mirth. Dear

Devon. He still had a trick or two up his sleeve, at that, and no wonder he had never been too concerned about the frivolous Miss Beckett's designs upon him . . .

"Well," said Caroline quickly, gathering up her skirts. "I must run. *Scores* of things to do, you know. We will call for you in our carriage." She stopped and giggled. "That way Lady Marbrough cannot keep you home on the pretense you have no proper escort!"

Annabelle saw her to the door, somewhat cheered by a mental picture of Devon, as grave as a headstone, describing to the meanest detail the poverty of existence Caroline would be expected to share as his wife . . . He was quite fortunate, at that, that Caro had not swooned in his arms!

And then, as the door closed behind her visitor, she felt the mirth drying away into something which brought a yearning to her chest too intense for tears. At least he had done Caroline the courtesy of a formal good-bye call.

To bolster her courage, Annabelle donned the adored rose gown for the evening. Around her throat Lady Marbrough clasped a necklace of shimmering diamonds, and Annabelle's eyes stung with gratitude for the gesture. She had made a friend of this lady while she was here, and she would not wish to see her hurt any more than she would Lucy or her own aunt . . . And in only a matter of hours the matter would be decided.

Bravely, she put her half-masque in place and bade Lady Marbrough an affectionate good night.

At first it seemed that Caroline's predictions of misconduct might prove to be correct. Arriving somewhat late at Bertie's town house, Annabelle walked into a veritable plethora of bejeweled and bemasqued ladies and gentlemen, all throwing themselves into the spirit of the confusion with gay laughter and high spirits. The orchestra played a lilting tune, dancers performed reels and waltzes indiscriminately, wine flowed freely. Annabelle could not help notice one or two couples, as the evening progressed, leave the festivities to wander among the darkened gardens, and she grew tense. If there were chaperones, they were very well hidden.

But she had no trouble at all recognizing Bertram, though his face was hidden by a wicked scarlet domino, and neither did he miss her. Immediately as she arrived, he took her arm and led her into the dance. "You see, Miss Arnsworth," he declared, "how very adept I am at penetrating disguises!"

"Indeed," she replied coolly, "and was that particular ability of yours ever intended to be kept secret?"

He threw back his head and laughed, and the gleam of his white teeth beneath the blood-red masque was somehow sinister. "I beg you, fair lady—this is to be a night of intrigue and *amour*—let us not tell all of our secrets at once!"

"Intrigue, perhaps," she responded. "*Amour*, never."

And his dark eyes sparked wickedly into hers. "Ah," he said softly. "But the night is young."

Annabelle attached herself to Caroline as desperately

as a drowning man might clutch at straws. And Caroline's protection was precisely as useful as that proverbial straw.

"Lucretia?" Caroline giggled, peering into Annabelle's eyes. "It *is* Lucretia, isn't it?"

"Yes," answered Annabelle nervously. "It is I."

Caroline pretended to pout and tapped Annabelle's arm playfully with her fan. "You are no fun at all! You're not supposed to tell, even if I guess. And anyone could tell it was you, anyway! You are not wearing your masque properly."

"Really, Caro, don't you believe this is all rather silly—"

But Caroline hushed her and took Annabelle's arm, lowering her voice into its common conspiratorial tones. "Do you see that gentleman over there? No, silly—*there!* He is staring directly at us."

Annabelle found the character Caroline referred to, who, though his face was obscured by a black domino, was staring at her quite boldly.

"He has been watching you all evening, and when I danced with him a moment ago he asked who you were! Of course I protested I did not know, but I think he means to come over to you."

Annabelle inquired curiously, "Who is he?"

Caroline lifted her shoulders. "I do not know."

Annabelle stared at her, aghast. "Caro! You mean you actually danced with a man you did not even know? Why—why, he could be anyone! Some dreadful friend of Mr. Dosset's or—anyone!"

But Caroline only shrugged again and laughed gaily.

"I have danced with a great many gentlemen tonight I do not know and intend to dance with a great many more! Oh, Lucretia, don't be such a spoilsport. Enjoy yourself!" And she left her friend with a cheerful wave, alone and unprotected.

If Annabelle had thought Bertram might soon put an end to her misery, she was very much mistaken. He was playing her along as the gods did Tantalus, prolonging the agony, giving no hint of what it was exactly that he had in store for her. By half past eleven her nerves were strung so tightly they must surely pop, and she was just beginning to have wild thoughts about slipping out and fleeing down the street to the safety of Lady Marbrough's home, when he approached her.

He bowed low. "Our dance, I believe."

They were playing a waltz.

She snapped open her fan and replied, "Thank you, I do not waltz."

He laughed and swept her into the dance so abruptly that she had no chance to protest. "Do not be absurd, dear thing! You are ruined already—or you will be before this night is over. Enjoy it while you can!"

Her hand tightened in fury on his shoulder and she looked directly into his repulsive eyes. "Don't you think you have played your disgusting little game quite long enough, Mr. Dosset?" she said in a low voice. "Are you not by now prepared for the finale?"

His teeth gleamed nastily as he whirled her around. "Oh, but I was assured you would enjoy being mystified as much as you enjoy mystifying others. Can I have been mistaken?"

"You have overrated yourself, Mr. Dosset," she replied. "Your mystification is quite transparent. I have known from the outset exactly how you intend to expose me—at the stroke of midnight when the masques are removed. I am only faintly curious as to why."

He looked at her in genuine astonishment. "Expose you? Why, my dear girl, my intention is nothing of the sort! That would be *quite* self-defeating, I assure you."

She found herself floundering, truly taken aback. "Then—what?"

He waltzed her off the floor and into a recessed alcove before she knew what he was about. When he looked down at her, the confident, calculating light in his eyes was quite terrifying.

He said smoothly, "As I see you are baffled, allow me to explain the whole to you. It has been my intention," he went on casually, "for some time now, to marry the very desirable Lucretia Arnsworth. You may have heard that my, er, circumstances, make such an alliance most appealing. The only difficulty was," he mused, "that the eminent Miss Arnsworth would have nothing to do with me, and neither would her disgracefully protective mother. You cannot imagine my relief when the solution to my problem walked into Lady Marbrough's parlor in the person of yourself."

Annabelle stared at him, her hands growing cold and the dancers whirling about her like masqued faces in a nightmare. She said, "But—I do not understand—"

"Of course you do, my dear," he crooned, and one hand came up to lightly trail beneath the pouf of sleeve at her shoulder. She could not bear the touch and jerked automatically away. He went on, undisturbed, "This very night will find you and me on our way to Gretna Green. By tomorrow morning all Brighton will know of our elopement and"—he snapped his fingers once—"for me, instant fortune. For Miss Arnsworth, wedded bliss."

Almost, a bubble of relief burst through her at the absurdity of this plan, but relief was shadowed by a stab of alarm which would never completely leave her as long as she was in his presence. "But that is quite ridiculous," she protested. "You know I am not Lucretia Arnsworth—what earthly good would it do you to marry me?"

He gave a short, ugly bark of laughter. "Marry you? Lord, no! But when the news is broadcast that Miss Arnsworth has eloped with me, she will have but one chance to save her reputation—and that is by making the deed a fact, by marrying me as quickly and as quietly as possible. She may as well, you see, for no other man will be likely to make her an offer within her lifetime, she would bring her poor mother into scandal and ruin . . . and, well, it is all very simple, don't you see?"

"It is insane!" she hissed violently, and her eyes were only two black sheets of horror behind the masque.

"It is extremely practical," he assured her, with a light tap of his hand upon her arm. "Now, at the stroke of midnight, you will leave the party to await me in the gazebo. We will make our departure before the unmasking is done. By the time supper is over our absence will undoubtedly be remarked and—*voilà!* A deed well done!"

She stared at him as he turned to go in increasing incredulity. "You cannot think that I will deliver myself so meekly into your hands!"

He glanced at her uninterestedly. "I do not see that it is a matter for debate. If you do not, you know that I will expose you, and that will ruin both you and Miss Arnsworth quite as effectively as if she were to refuse to marry me after our elopement becomes known. I am merely offering you both a graceful way to solve all our problems."

It was quite incredible, of course. Annabelle watched him go with a relief which was only slightly shot through by fear. It was totally unworkable and unthinkable and she had far overestimated his powers of discernment if he thought for one moment she would calmly agree to such a wild scheme. For one thing, he had overlooked the fact that her great affection for Lucretia would not allow her to commit her so cruelly into the hands of a man such as Bertram Dosset, no matter what the consequences. For another, his plan simply would not work, because . . . because he did not know that at this moment the real Lucretia Arnsworth was being fêted throughout the countryside on her engagement to the good Freddy, and should such a wild rumor of elopement arise, it would be *he* who was ruined, not Lucretia. For there was no chance at all in his ever convincing anyone that it was true. No chance at all.

But it was up to Annabelle to persuade him of that fact, and to do it in such a manner that he would at the same time see the folly in exposing her charade. She would bluff him with the truth.

But, as she waited in the darkened gazebo as the hour

approached midnight, the music and the laughter from the opened windows reaching her with an eerie quality across the lawn upon a light breeze, she could not prevent the knots in her stomach from tightening into cold lumps of pure fear. She was dealing with a dangerous man here, and a desperate one, and what if she were unable to persuade him of his folly? She would kick, bite, and scream, if necessary, she decided grimly. The threat of exposure meant nothing to her now in the face of this new, more horrible threat. And Bertram Dosset would *not* have the best of her this night!

She had discarded her mask upon the gazebo seat and busied herself by twisting her fingers together back and forth nervously. When she heard footsteps approach upon the gravel walk she leaped to her feet and her heart did one terrible cascade of fear, she calmed herself forcefully and waited for him.

The dancing light from the windows played for a moment on the scarlet mask as he came up the steps, and then he was inside the white fretwork structure, lost in shadows. She began quickly, before he could speak, "Mr. Dosset, I would have you know that I am here for only one reason, and that is to attempt to dissuade you from this impossible folly."

He said nothing, and over the lawn the notes of the supper waltz reached her.

She went on, "I would also have you know that nothing you can do—no threats you can make—seems more abhorrent to me than what you have just suggested, so you may feel free to do your worst if you are so inclined when I am finished."

Her hands were clasped together so tightly that they were becoming numb, but she went on, her voice steady and calm, "It was, as you know, my cousin Lucretia who received the invitation to join Lady Marbrough in Brighton. Lucretia persuaded me to come in her stead because we do rather resemble one another and she felt it necessary to stay at home to—foster a developing relationship she had with a young gentleman in the vicinity. What you do not know, Mr. Dosset, is that since that time, Lucretia has become engaged to that same young gentleman. So you see, I'm very much afraid your scheme has no chance of working. Lucretia could not marry you if she would, and no one will ever believe your tale."

In the silence, she thought she knew exactly what he was thinking. A broken engagement, an elopement in the night . . . the situation was, far from being a deterrent, precisely to his liking. Then I will kick and scream, thought Annabelle somewhat desperately. For he will not take me from this place . . .

Then he said, "Miss . . . ?" and hesitated politely.

She answered, "Morgan," and found she could say no more. Her courage had abruptly deserted her.

From across the lawn, wild shouts of laughter and discovery reached her as the clock struck midnight and masques were discarded. "Miss Morgan," he said and reached up to untie his masque. His voice was very quiet. "You are a fool."

The masque fell away.

For a moment everything whirled dizzily as he stepped out of the shadows, the scalloped patterns of the ceiling, the lights from distant windows, the music and the laughter and the cool, dark lawn. She must have swayed a little on her feet as her hand flew up to clutch at her throat, for abruptly his arm was about her waist, supporting her. "Devon!" she gasped.

Gently, he lowered her to the bench. "You are without a doubt," he returned gruffly, "the most foolhardy young lady I have ever met." His face was stern with anger, though that was denied by the softness in his eyes, but it did not matter. It would not have mattered had he come raging at her in a black fury, for only to have him there, to see his face and feel his strong arm about her . . .

"Have you any idea," he continued sternly, "what might have happened to you if it *had* been Dosset you met here and not myself? Have you completely taken leave of your senses?"

"Oh, Devon!" And abruptly bewilderment overcame all other emotions of relief and surprise and the love which was flooding through her, and she sat up straight. "But how did you know? Where is Mr. Dosset?"

He smiled grimly and patted her hand. "I had a feeling you weren't quite so capable of taking care of yourself as you would have me believe. Though when you did not wear my roses . . ."

She whispered numbly, "I thought they were from *him*."

He squeezed her hand with gentle understanding and went on, "I thought perhaps you did not desire my protection, but I made it my business to stay near you at all times. I overheard Dosset coercing you into this assignation, though I did not dream you would be so foolish as to come."

She said, "I had to try . . ." And then she looked at him in confusion. "But the masque—where *is* he? How—"

He smiled ruefully. "The estimable Mr. Dosset is at this moment cooling his temper in a not-so-distant duck pond. He will not bother you again, I assure you. I managed to persuade him to lend me this." He lifted the masque negligently.

She started to giggle, but then it was lost in the overwhelming import of new truths. She found she could no longer look at him. "So," she managed after a moment, "now you know—everything."

"Yes," he agreed gravely. "I suppose I do."

"You know," she had to say the words out loud, "that I am not who you have taken me for."

"Yes," was all he answered.

She went on, twisting her fingers again into tight little knots in her lap, "Annabelle Morgan is only a poor relation of Lucretia Arnsworth. She has not name or fortune and makes her living with a pen."

"Well, Miss Morgan," he said at last, heavily, "I suppose I owe you an apology."

Her eyes flew up to him. "You—?"

"Yes." His face was very sober. "You may recall one night more than a week ago—many things were said in the heat of passion, and, not knowing your true identity, I"—he glanced down—"Well, I am very much afraid that I must ask your forgiveness for my behavior, in leading you to think things that were not strictly true.

You see, at that time—as well as now—my affections were already engaged."

Her lips parted on a still breath, her eyes fixed on his wide and immobile, and she felt as though the very center of the earth had fallen away beneath her feet. She only stared.

"You see," he went on gently, and slowly his hand came up to cup her face. "I made my proposal to Lucretia Arnsworth, while in fact I was really in love with one entrancing Miss Morgan."

Before a single cry of joy could escape her lips, his own had smothered them with a deep and lingering kiss. And through the passion which swelled within her, through the whirling delight and breathless ecstasy, a single thought rose to cool her. She broke away. "You left me," she accused. "That night—when you discovered about my book . . ."

He let her go only to the distance which would allow him to hold her shoulders, and now the expression on his face was genuine. "For that I do sincerely apologize," he said softly. "My behavior on that occasion was truly inexcusable. I was stunned, and I acted in a very childish fashion. By the next day, of course, I had realized my error and was on my way to beg your forgiveness—when the news of my uncle's death arrived."

She sat up straight, her own petty sorrows forgotten. "His death! Oh, Devon, I am sorry!"

He nodded, and his eyes were sad. "It was expected, of course, but never welcome. At any rate," he turned back to her, "I never intended to be away so long, but the estate was quite a good bit more entangled than I imagined, with first one thing and then the other and, of course, the confusion in ascertaining his brother's demise . . ."

She looked at him, hardly daring to hope. "So he *is* deceased? You are the heir?"

He nodded. "He has been all these years, and my uncle's solicitors informed me they were instructed to keep the information from me. I suppose it was my uncle's way of ascertaining my true loyalty."

"Oh, Devon, I am so pleased for you! I know it is what you most wanted in the world, to live your life there . . ."

"No," he corrected, taking her hands. "What I most wanted in the world was you."

She blushed and replied softly, "Then I am yours."

He brought her fingers swiftly to his lips, and then, as though fearing that that simple gesture might lead to something more, he went on, "There was one happy note, however, which I think might have rather pleased Lucretia Arnsworth, though I am not so certain about the penniless Miss Morgan."

She looked at him curiously. "What?"

He laughed suddenly and lightly. "Have you ever thought, my dear, how much distress would have been avoided if I had only known from the beginning that you had no more of a fortune than I? I would not have been afraid to love you then . . ."

"Devon, you are not being clear."

He looked at her, his eyes twinkling. "The old rascal had invested thousands on the 'Change, years ago. I never knew anything of it at all, and, I rather think, that in his failing years, he forgot all about it. At any rate, he has not precisely amassed a huge fortune, but it will be enough for me to put the estate back in working order and restore the manor . . ."

"Oh, Devon!"

"And," he added, drawing her gently into his arms, "to allow me to support a wife in a manner similar to that to which she has grown accustomed."

Again, only a sigh, "Oh, Devon!"

For a time they merely rested in one another's arms, content in their happiness, listening to the gentle music which floated across the lawn and to the rhythm of their own hearts in unison. Then Devon said thoughtfully, one hand entwining in her curls, "One thing does concern me, though. You have so many identities— Lucretia Arnsworth, Miss Morgan, Mr. A. P. Morgan, and soon Mrs. Devon Lanson—what if I should forget and hail you in public by the wrong name? How dreadfully embarrassing."

She glanced up to catch the teasing light in his eyes and then snuggled once again securely in his arms. "For now," she sighed contentedly, "call me Annabelle."